FOX
COURT MARTIAL

by
Adam Hardy

PINNACLE BOOKS • NEW YORK CITY

This is a work of fiction. All the characters and events portrayed in this book are fictional, and any resemblance to real people or incidents is purely coincidental.

FOX: COURT MARTIAL

Copyright © 1974 by Adam Hardy

A Pinnacle Books edition, published by special arrangement with New English Library Limited, London.

ISBN: 0-523-00505-9

First printing, December 1974

Printed in the United States of America

PINNACLE BOOKS, INC.
275 Madison Avenue
New York, N.Y. 10016

COURT MARTIAL

CHAPTER ONE

Fox heard the clash of iron at his back and swung about instantly on the threshold of the cell to grip the rough iron bars. They still vibrated. That sound—that diabolical sound of barred iron clashing together—that confounded damned sound rang in his head. That dreadful sound of iron-barred gates closing in on a man and shutting him away, that sound was the same in every prison in the whole world, booming and reverberating and without mercy.

Fox's brown calloused hands with the blunt and ragged fingernails clenched on the black-painted iron, scaled and harsh. He glared out on the escort who had brought him here.

The young lieutenant with his file of marines saw Fox's face and his hand dropped instinctively to his sword hilt. Fox did not miss the sideways fleeting look in the man's eyes, the hesitancy, the shock.

The turnkey jangled his keys on their enormous ring. The lock thunked like a thirty-two pounder. Orders bawled in the close stone corridor, chasing the echoes of the clanging iron bars up deafeningly in the confined space. The marines tramped off. The turnkey went with them, his keys a jangling counter-point to their footsteps on the cold stones. The officer looked back, once. Not one of them had said a word.

Almost—almost—George Abercrombie Fox shouted after them: "And sod you too, Jack!"

But he did not. He had no heart in it.

1

After all he had done, after all the effort and the blood and the gallantry—the gallantry of his men— here he was, flung into a prison cell. That this was what he had expected, symbolically, at the least, did nothing to satisfy his savage feelings. But symbols were too frail when it came to handling George Abercrombie Fox. He had no ship at the moment and there was no captain in Port Mahon who would take him under his wing so instead of a gentlemanly confinement in a wardroom awaiting his trial he was thumped down here. All strictly according to the book; but had he been an honourable or a gilded scion of the nobility room would have been found for him elsewhere. As it was, even the friendly family of Spaniards Captain the Honourable Percy Staunton had settled him with, had been unable to keep him in their pleasant villa once he had recovered from his wounds.

As he stood there, squat, chunky, unlovely, incredibly coarse, gripping onto the cold iron bars, despair threatened to overwhelm Fox. He could never be disillusioned, for he had never cherished illusions; he could never be cowed for he would curse and fight until they sewed him up in a hammock with a thirty-two pounder roundshot for company; but this queasy kind of treacherous black despair would sometimes descend on him with the knowledge of his own insignificance. He would fight and struggle for that was Foxey's way; but all the time he thus raved and struck out he wondered if there was any rhyme or reason to it all. Only his family of Foxes by the Thames could hold him to what he conceived of as his duty. But for them he might have acted as any other man, and despaired utterly, and given up, and been crushed.

Slowly he forced himself to unclench those gripping talons of his and release the iron bars. He stared about the stone cell. It was just a prison cell. He had been

2

brought here in readiness for the court martial from the house of Salvator Hernando. Hernando, although Spanish, got on well with the English sailors and Captain Staunton had had no difficulty in persuading him to take in and care for the wounded Lieutenant Fox. Fox had not gone to the hospital on the island, and for that he was grateful.

Once again he was fit and well, raging to get to sea doing all the things he did so superlatively well, roaring to scoop his greedy fists into Prize Money.

Instead of all that, here he was, incarcerated.

For a sailor with the sea breeze in his nostrils and the sea itself in his veins, this was as vile a fate as any that could be imagined.

He understood only too well the British sailorman's ready acceptance of a flogging instead of being shut up in prison.

Being G. A. Fox he felt absolute confidence he could break out of this prison cell.

Had this been a French prison, one of the malodorous hellholes like Verdun or Valincent, for instance, or a Spanish inquisition-damned pesthole, he would have been up and active and about his business of breaking in a few heads and breaking out of the stone walls and iron bars.

But this was a British prison, a British naval prison.

The difference dampened all his fire and resolution.

If he broke out and escaped he would then be condemned. He would have to turn pirate, as he had nearly done already, and go aroving in the Med. The life would be brisk and hearty for a space, and then he'd dance on air at the end of it, just like his uncle Abercrombie who had danced that merry little hempennoosed jig from Tyburn Tree.

Very down, very depressed, very beaten, then felt George Abercrombie Fox in those moments. He heard

3

the distant clanging of iron bars ringing and reverberating along the stone corridor, and then the heavy rhythmic stamp of booted feet. So they were coming for him. Someone—he felt almost certain it was that tearaway Mr. Midshipman Grey—had left a new set of clothing for him, which he had donned when he left his sick bed. A new blue jacket, very smart with its white lieutenant's edging, white breeches and silk stockings—silk stockings!—and a pair of shoes that fitted him tolerably well. Master's Mate Carker had hung onto the five-ball sword presented to him by Lord Kintlesham in those heady days when Fox had been betrothed to the noble lord's fat and somehow pathetic daughter, Sophie. Mr. Carker had cherished that sword, Fox realised now, simply because Fox had shouted coarsely at him not to drop it into the drink. Fox would be given the sword just prior to the court-martial, only to have it taken away from him immediately in the ritual that must have been as old as Noah and the troubles he had with his animal crew.

The crash of the marine party approached. The lieutenant was the same one. He eyed Fox askance.

Fox waited for him to speak.

Truth to tell, Fox felt like lying down and going to sleep. He felt like giving up. He'd done deeds that should have brought him diamond-hilted swords of honour, an earldom, the thanks of both Houses of Parliament, posting to the choicest French frigate captured, everything on which his heart was set for the good of his family; instead, he'd been rewarded by incarceration, arrest and the promise of a court-martial for his life.

The young lieutenant moistened his lips. He started to speak twice, fluffed his words, and started over.

At last he got out: "Captain Copeland has just

quitted his anchorage. *Sybil* has been ordered to Palermo."

Clearly, the lieutenant thought this news meant a great deal to Fox. Fox knew Captain Copeland slightly, and he did admit to annoyance that the captain had been despatched at this time so that he would not be available to sit on the end of the row of judges who would condemn Fox, for Fox fancied Copeland might understand.

The lieutenant blundered on.

"There are only four ships with post captains over three year's seniority in Mahon now—"

Fox understood.

To constitute a legal court martial five post captains were required. Oh, yes, Fox was well enough aware of the special provisions which gave summary powers to commanders in chief to convene a court martial with less. He doubted if those provisions need apply now, with ships of the Royal Navy constantly on the move in the Mediterranean as they sought to hold onto the tenuous power the victory of the Nile had won for England. Fox knew his way about the jagged-edged regulations governing the navy. As any honest sailorman did he detested the smart sea-lawyer. Staring at this neat young popinjay of a lieutenant Fox felt the thin gash across his face itching, his boiled-leather lips quivering into his ghastly semblance of a smile. George Abercrombie Fox an honest sailorman! The idea that he was honest enough to detest a man trying to prove by the authority's own orders and regulations a right made Fox grimace horribly.

The lieutenant swallowed. "The papers have been withdrawn, Mr. Fox. The court will be reconvened when a sufficiency of post captains is present in Port Mahon."

Fox said: "And?"

"And meanwhile you will remain under confinement."

Fox did not say: "Bigod I won't! Not me! Not Foxey!"

Instead he let out a long moaning sigh. He clutched the white linen shirt beneath the white-bordered blue jacket. He groaned and then retched a little. He slid down the iron bars. He lay on the floor. The stone was damned hard and uncomfortable and he turned himself over with a fine free kick of his legs much after the fashion of a landsman he had seen have convulsions, wriggled, made himself as comfortable as he could on the cell floor.

Damned blagskites! Going to keep him shut up down here in the bowels of the earth, were they? Well, they knew what bowels were for and they knew what Fox was, and he intended to take the next step in nature's wonderful process.

He gargled and spluttered and let out a yell, followed by: "The pain! The pain! I need a doctor— *dottore!* I'm going—I'm going—"

If he had overdone it the young lieutenant who probably only needed to shave once a week could not tell. Fox let his eyes—both of which were behaving beautifully—flick along the row of marines' faces. Every face might have been carved from a lump of English oak. Well. If they so much as blinked they'd be triced up and the cat would teach them to behave.

"Sergeant!" cried the lieutenant. He said sergeant, and not sar'nt, which showed how green he was. "Fetch a doctor. God bless my soul! Mr. Fox is taken poorly."

"Air!" yelled Fox, and remembered to gargle and thrash around a trifle. "Air! Sunshine! I'm going— going—"

"And, sergeant!" shrilled the lieutenant. "My compliments to Captain Prothero. Tell him what's hap-

6

pened here—'pon my soul, Mr. Fox will have to be taken up."

Aye, Fox considered, many a good man had been taken up in this life.

Goddammittohell! He must be getting really light-headed!

Fox stuck up a right arm that quivered. His brown iron-hard hand unclenched and his broad and powerful fingers spread and groped and fastened on the thigh of the lieutenant who bent over him. He gripped. The lieutenant squealed.

"Air! Sunshine! My wounds—battle, fire, sudden death! I must be going—"

Those found guilty by a court martial and sentenced to death were usually hanged at the yard-arm. Although Fox could feel the senseless comedy of the situation, and that itch still afflicted his lips, he knew the stakes he was playing for here. If they were going to hang him—and they could, they could—he'd make them fight every damned inch of the way.

By the time the doctor trotted down, the young lieutenant's pimply face had been stricken by the horror of Fox's plight. He confirmed that Mr. Fox would clearly expire if he was not taken to the hospital at once.

"I'll decide on that, young man, if ye please!"

The doctor, elderly, testy, balding, wasn't going to have some young whipper-snapper fresh out from England showing him his professional duty. Fox had to organise the doctor, quickly.

The doctor's black sleeve ended in a frayed edge, and a stringy but muscular wrist extended beyond that, close up to Fox's eyes as the doctor prodded his chest.

With a motion at once fluidly quick and yet precisely timed and aimed, Fox bent and bit into the

7

doctor's wrist as though he was taking a chunk from a good Kent apple.

The doctor let out a scream of agony.

Fox jerked back before the man's instinctive reaction could rip out his teeth.

"By God! The bastard bit me!"

"He is unwell, doctor—" The lieutenant believed.

Captain Prothero, a vast bulk of scarlet and white and gold, with black boots in which Fox's face showed almost as uglily in reflection as it was in truth, bent down.

"Get him up," he growled. "Sar'nt! Snap to it!"

"My arm!" The doctor's face had turned a corroded green in the lantern-light. "Venom! He's mad! I'll have to take my arm off! The tar-tub!" He ran out, yelling.

Fox gargled and let his head dangle as the marines lifted him. They carried him out of the cell and up the stone stairs and out into God's sunlight.

Had he been a common sailorman, a pressed-man, a Quota Man, an able-seaman, even, they'd simply have chained him up to the wall and stuffed a leather gag into his mouth and left him down there to rot. He could feel no shame that as an officer he rated better treatment than the men. He knew what the lower deck was like, for wasn't he a Thames marshboy who'd jumped up through the hawsehole to all the glory of the quarterdeck? No matter that the hands held him in contempt, no matter that his superior officers held him in contempt; he, G. A. Fox, was an officer, and to hell with 'em all!

There was some confusion as to where he should be sent and Prothero wanted to despatch him to the island hospital; in the end they checked his papers and agreed to send him back to the house of Salvator Hernando. He'd lain there sick before; he might do so again. The

8

naval commandant agreed. It would not be for long, for ships continually came and went and Mahon was a busy place. Admiral Nelson, although based on Palermo—and that was a scandal that delighted the Fleet—had been through and might be through again. There would be post captains aplenty then.

Aware of the frightful risks he was running, for a mad lieutenant would never be treated with the same kind of leniency as a mad captain, Fox was content to let them trundle him up to Don Salvator's pleasantly airy villa. Doña Isabella greeted with much fluttering of hands and scarves and eyebrows this return of the wounded hero. Fox had no graces he cared to exhibit; but he was conscious on this occasion of the rather tattered label of 'hero' pinned onto his bosom by the words of his hands and of Grey and Carker. And, no doubt also, Captain Staunton had put in the few necessary good words. Fox disliked the hero concept; but he recognised its validity, indeed its importance, in war time. He subjected himself to the Hernando ministrations.

Don Salvator seemed to Fox to regard Captain Staunton with the reverence of an acolyte for the temple image, as his saviour as much as friend, and given the political climate this could easily be so. Staunton, as a young man with very high connections, commanded the respect that was so unthinkingly given, and as unthinkingly denied to men like Fox.

"Captain Staunton was desolated he could not take you with him, Mr. Fox." Don Salvator's English was idiomatically very good, marred only by a thick accent. Fox's own perfect Castilian he preferred not to utilise, for various deep and devious reasons habitual to him. "The beautiful *Furieuse* made a delightful sight as she sailed out."

Well.

9

Of course.

The details were quickly ascertained. Captain the Honourable Percy Staunton had stood his court martial and had been honourably acquitted. His ship, H.M. frigate *Pylas* had fought a swarm of scoundrelly French gunboats to a standstill and had sunk with colours flying. The butcher's bill had been heavy. Captain Staunton had made his way back to Minorca in ship's boats towing rafts crowded with his wounded. Yes, it made a fine stirring story. There was no mention in that story of Lieutenant Fox's part or, incredibly enough considering her size alone, of *Princessa Cristina Maria*.

Fox was quite accustomed to that sort of treatment, it was what he had reluctantly come to expect in his naval life; but for some reason now evidently best forgotten, he had thought Percy Staunton, for all his chinless, flap-eared, nincompoopery, to be a cut above the usual run of aristocratic bunglers and office-chasers. Well, the report Fox had written out with so much painstaking care to find just the right words to cloak what he had been really up to had been sent in, and that, indeed, carried word of the big Spanish three-decker. He would just have to continue to school himself as he had done all his twenty-four years at sea.

He really had to think of what defence he would put up at his court martial. He would call Grey and Carker as witnesses, of course, as well as Hogan the carpenter and Joachim the gunner's mate. He made out a list of his witnesses in readiness for the deputy judge-advocate of the fleet. He would have called Staunton, of course; but now that fortunate young man had been given the plum command of a fine captured French frigate and was off on a cruise, that was out of the question.

He learned also that Commander Sanders, that fat-

10

faced, blue-eyed, jolly captain of the brig *Raccoon* had also been blessed with command, and had gone about the navy's business. Evidently, during Sanders' court martial he had been blown up into the hero-mould for sailing a captured French open boat back from the island where *Raccoon* had foundered. Well, Fox might have a few words to say on that score.

During the days that passed Fox found he did not need to worry as he had thought. He could easily prove that he had not deserted *Raccoon*. The contrary was the case, despite that, a court martial had pronounced a verdict of honourable acquittal on Commander Sanders. All the old Raccoons who had sailed with him on their subsequent fantastic return voyage would speak up for him. They'd show the public—aye! and the Navy—just what Commander bloody Richard bloody Sanders had done; too right they would.

The thought of Sanders being asked why he had taken the beached French boat from the island and pushed off and left Fox and the men with him made Fox's thin lips rick back. He was never a one to take an insult lying down if he could get up and kick back —preferably low—or one to forget a grudge.

From the high perch of Don Salvator Hernando's villa it was possible to see only a small part of the vast anchorage serving Port Mahon. A couple of frigates swung to their moorings down there, and these must house the two men who would sit with another three on judgment on him. When he questioned Don Salvator he received a piece of unwelcome news.

"Captain Lanchester, of *Sea Foam,* Mr. Fox. A very fine gentleman, indeed, for he has two mistresses here, everyone knows, and already he ogles the good Mrs. Pratt, wife of the commissary."

"Sounds a likely sort," commented Fox. "The other, for, sink me, I'm hanged if I recognise her."

"*Lynx*, Mr. Fox. Her commander is Captain Stone." Hernando licked his lips. "Such a grand gentleman."

"Stone," said Fox. His cuttingly keen memory, so damned retentive, stirred. "Would that be Lemuel Stone?"

"Si, Mr. Fox. Captain Lemuel Stone. You perhaps know him?"

"Not Captain Stone, Don Salvator. I knew him when he was Midshipman Stone."

Hernando glanced away from Fox's face, and again he licked his lips. He started to say something, and changed his mind, and passed some nondescript comment.

Stone!

Fox could expect nothing but the blackest animosity from Stone—Toady Stone, the mids in the old *Nicodemus* had called him. Toady Stone, who had sucked up to Captain Cuthbert Rowlands until even that gentlemanly sailor had sickened. No, Lieutenant Fox could expect from Captain Stone in memory of old times no mercy whatsoever.

But what the hell! The facts were there. His men would speak out, they'd simply say what had happened, and the court would have to see he had done all that a British sailor should do—aye, and more.

Then, casually, out of the blue, Don Salvator let rip the broadside that sank all Fox's hopes.

". . . *Furieuse*, so fine and handsome a ship for the dear Captain Staunton. He was most pleased he could ship all the men who were with you, Mr. Fox. He asked me to say how pleased he was with the men's bearing, and Mr. Grey and Mr. Carker are a great boon in his new command."

Fox listened and the lines on his face gouged in deeper into that weatherbeaten gargoyle. Staunton had taken all his witnesses! Now there was no one to prove

12

his case. Completely alone, he must walk into the court and face his accusers and his judges—and they would find him guilty and break him and have him hung from the yard-arm—and then—he could be hung, drawn and quartered. He could. He could. He could . . .

CHAPTER TWO

George Abercrombie Fox stood in great peril of his life.

That was no new experience. But, whereas previously he had risked that obstinate neck of his in hurricane and fire and lee shores, facing the smoking mouths of enemy guns, storming up ramparts against enemy muskets and bayonets, now he stood in dire peril from his own countrymen and all the cold machinery of naval law.

Everything was done with due respect for order.

There existed a style in these things, and that style was punctiliously maintained no matter if the proceedings took place aboard a ship anchored in some sweltering foreign port instead of Spithead.

A fighting sailor grew inured to the idea that some day a flying chunk of langridge might chew his tripes out; but the idea of being skewered by a Latin tag horrified him far more profoundly.

Now that all the old Raccoons had been swept up to serve in Staunton's spanking *Furieuse,* Fox was left entirely alone and unsupported. He could not bring a single witness to prove his claims as set out in his report. This was a body blow. The court had already ruled on Commander Sanders and his actions had brought forth approbation. Now this miserable jumped-up Lieutenant Fox had blown in and was putting everything in doubt. Sanders, so this madman Fox claimed, had deliberately left his first lieutenant and a goodly portion of his crew on the island. He had, in effect, marooned them.

Fox eyed the plump and pretty serving wench, Rosaria of the low neckline and the twinkling ankles, and swore and went back to figuring out just what he could say when those goldlaced authorities accused him of cowardice and desertion in the face of the enemy.

This was no cut-and-dried court martial. Every captain must be tried on the loss of his command. Well, Fox had not been in command and was not being tried for that. There was no question whatsoever of his entering the court with the comfortable knowledge that the whole proceedings were merely formal, part of naval tradition, and that at the end the president might say something like: "Your conduct, together with that of the officers and men under your command, reflects not only the highest honour on you, Mr. Fox, but on the whole of His Majesty's navy. You are therefore most honourably acquitted."

Oh, no.

What the president might say, what he could say, might end with: ". . . and there be hung, and drawn, and quartered." Only he'd wrap it up in legal jargon to disguise the smell of blood and drown the yells that Fox knew he'd let rip, God help him.

He went over in his mind everything that had happened since that fool Macbridge, Master of *Raccoon*, had taken her so confidently into the cove and ripped her bottom out. The events danced before him in a macabre succession. Every now and then a scarlet image from Acre would drop over his memory, and he'd curse, and shake his head, and push it away. For Acre belonged to a time that appeared so long ago— when he had been in temporary command of *Raccoon* and betrothed to Sophie, only daughter of Lord

15

Kintlesham, and had seemed well on the way to that beautiful swab on his shoulder.

Lemuel Stone.

As a midshipman Stone had been vicious, cowardly, arrogant; he must have overcome his cowardice now, else he would never command one of his Britannic Majesty's frigates. But, for the rest . . . Fox sweated out his time of ordeal, his days in the desert, as he waited for the first ship to sail into Port Mahon bringing with her the fifth post captain to sit in judgment on him.

His chief comfort during this time came from the excellent copies of Molière in Don Salvator's small but select library. Fox read in the original French with keen delight, savouring every nuance, every jest, winkling out the deep and devious interplay of character and motive. Old Molière really knew what made people tick. He had them off pat. So Fox sat in a window seat in the sunshine as the year drew on and read his beloved Molière and waited for that fifth post captain to arrive.

Don Salvator's occasional visitors found this craggy lieutenant with the massively weather-beaten face reticent, taciturn, withdrawn and they put this down to his impending court martial. That was enough to make any man's mind congeal. Far from congealing, Fox's mind was a quick-silver broth of schemes and plans. If he was found guilty he'd have to crack the guard on the head and dive overboard. He'd stand no chance once they had him firmly in their clutches as a condemned man. He could steal a boat, he could smash down any opposition unlucky enough to cross his path. After that—well, his fragile plans to become a pirate would have to be implemented.

Where this would leave his family he did not care to dwell on. They depended on him. Oh, yes, Archie tried

16

to bring in money from time to time; but he still cherished his revolutionary leanings—how they'd planned in the old days of the L.C.S.!—and was virtually unemployable. Bert was serving under Captain Rupert Colborn of the Forty Third—and that reminded Fox that he hadn't heard from Rupert, the one man outside the family he could call friend—for far too long. He fretted that Rupert and Bert were all right, still living; even, perhaps lying wounded and festering. Phantasms tortured Fox to add to the devils prodding him with pitch forks with each tine labelled Court Martial.

Of the younger children that fiery tear away Ebeneezer had taken himself off and no-one had heard a word of him in years. He'd be—Fox calculated—yes, Ebeneezer would be about twenty-six now. The maniac was probably living as high as a duke on ill-gotten gains, or had been hanged at Tyburn, like his uncle Abercrombie.

Strange—Bert who was a serving soldier was two years younger than Ebeneezer. The eldest daughter of the Fox family, Susan, was following the traditional path and remained at home by the Thames to care for her mother, the family and the house their money could afford. As for Alice—Fox wasn't sure just what she would do and hoped she would make a good marriage. Prostitution lay in wait for girls as a life into which it was all too easy to slip.

The youngest, young Charlotte, who must be nineteen now, only wanted to sing and dance and turn cartwheels, as Fox remembered her, and he hadn't been home since before *Duchess*.

No—clearly, George Abercrombie Fox could not allow himself to be hanged at the yard-arm. If guilty, he must escape. Then he would fabricate some outlandish way of sending the proceeds of his piracy home to his family.

Yes.

That was settled.

That night, as though everything was over, he tumbled Rosaria of the low neck-line and the twinkling ankles, and she laughed and giggled and egged him on, until he lay back, one hand trailing across her bare stomach, feeling more peaceful than he had in weeks. He spoke the Catalan of the islands perfectly.

She pushed herself up on an elbow and leaned over him so that her black hair hung down and her soft plump breasts swung against his face in the dim moonlit chamber.

"And are you finished already, Englishman?"

"Bigod," said G. A. Fox. "That's a challenge I've never resisted yet." And he seized her and upended her and as she shrieked in delighted alarm he showed her if an honest sailorman could ever be finished.

Just why he always seemed to attract the most unlikely women with this damned charisma of his he didn't know, nor in moments like this did he much care. He had a face like a weatherbeaten old figurehead and eyes that pierced a sham or a charade in a person's character like grape from a sixty-eight pounder carronade shredding sailcloth. He was a brusque, damn-you-to-hell, pickled in salt old tarpaulin; yet there were men in the British Navy he knew without question would follow him into the cannon's mouth. He gave the luscious Rosaria a final slap on a cheeky rump and tumbled her out of the bed and so spread his arms and legs wide over the twisted sheets and went to sleep. For Rosaria, the experience had been one she had never known before—such delight, such passion—such *force!* She would put cocky young Alfonso in his place next time, a simple hand move-

18

ment, thumb and little finger widely extended, would make him understand, and shrink.

The next day promised to be just like the one before, with the exception that the night might hold Rosaria. A cutter came in with news, relayed quickly enough through the channels of gossip by Hernando to Fox, that Commodore Duckworth was most likely to return to Minorca. He had, after all, helped in the capture of the place last year. All manner of exciting things were going on around the Mediterranean, with alarms and excursions that the French were once more at sea, there had been enormous illuminated processions and fêtes for Nelson—and coupled with his name always, now, was that of the Admiral's fancy, Lady Hamilton, Naples had been regained, Malta still held out against Ball, Nelson was now Duke of Bronte—wherever that was. The Turks and the Russians were kicking up trouble—and Fox remembered with what delicate and yet brutal effort he had pinched one such misunderstanding in the bud. Yes, things were happening, and here Lieutenant Fox lay mewed up awaiting court martial. He fretted so much Rosaria took pity on him three times before nightfall.

The next day—day after day after damned day— Fox was about to enter the long morning room when the voices of men in conversation halted him. He recognised Don Salvator, and the voices of two acquaintances, pale, colourless men. Riding powerfully over these polite tones came the blast of a rich and fruity port-wine voice, full of confidence and arrogance, full of the knowledge of self-importance.

Fox cocked his head.

Faint memories stirred. Allowing for age and the nearly twenty years that separated them—that might be the voice of Midshipman Lemuel Stone grown into Captain Lemuel Stone. Fox remained where he was.

19

"Damned disgrace!" The voice thundered on. "All Lord Nelson can do is hang around the skirts of that bitch of a whore! What are we doing? Chasing our tails around the Med when we should be at the Frogs! It won't do, sir, damme, it won't do."

Fox risked a look.

Yes—that florid complexion, that stout and robust frame, filled out now and paunchy, those dark and dangerous eyes—oh, yes, this was Toady Stone come into his heaven, with the two epaulettes on his shoulders glittering and proclaiming his glory in the morning sunshine.

"Troubridge keeps on at him, and if Lord Nelson don't take notice of Troubridge, then, damme, who will he take notice of? Lord Saint Vincent's gone back to England." Here Stone's voice bubbled with inner mirth. "But their Lordships ain't so far gone as to make Lord Nelson Commander-in-Chief. Bless my soul, no! He's only senior admiral." Fox took a last look. Stone appeared thoroughly satisfied with his own thoughts, although he expressed so much dissatisfaction. "Not while he toadies around that debased Neapolitan court. The King and Queen have driven him out of his senses. There is no captain more loyal than me. But there are limits, sir, there are limits."

Fox withdrew.

He had to withdraw.

Otherwise he would have stormed in and kicked Toady Stone up the bottom. How dare the bastard speak thus of Admiral Nelson? God knew, Fox distrusted and hated admirals as a tenet of existence; but Nelson was different. For his part, Fox, who had met Lady Hamilton and been vividly reminded of Kitty Higgins, would have welcomed the chance to jump into bed with the lady. If Nelson was making a fool of

20

himself, who in all the navy—all the world—had a better right?

Shortly thereafter and feeling thoroughly out of sorts, Fox had to compose himself as Don Salvator bustled through.

Stone had left.

"He tells me, my dear Mr. Fox, that his secretary is appointed with a warrant to act as deputy judge-advocate. A seventy-four is expected today, and to-morrow—" Hernando coughed, and tried to be delicate. "Tomorrow, my dear Mr. Fox—"

"They'll fire the gun and hoist the flag. I know."

"I am sure everything will turn out right for you. After what dear Captain Staunton said, and your men —why—it must be all right for you!"

"Except that Staunton and my hands aren't here."

Don Salvator coughed and went on: "Captain Stone was speaking of Admiral Nelson. Such a strange business. It seems that Admiral Nelson is persuaded that a course of electricity will improve the sight of his impaired eye. If the electrifying is good it might even restore the sight of his blind eye. Perhaps this—"

"I only hope it does," said Fox. He felt profoundly on the subject. In moments of action or lust or danger the sight of his own left eye closed up in that confounded ring of purple and black, and if the going became extraordinarily rough he lost the sight of his right eye, too, and went completely blind. He wished Nelson luck with his electrifying.

The next day His Britannic Majesty's seventy-four gun Ship of the Line *Balthazar* picked up her moorings and her canvas came down and was gathered in and the hands set to about the perennial tasks of the sailor in port.

Fox was standing in the window moodily looking out over the water, unable to see *Balthazar*, when he heard the doors at his back open. He heard footsteps. Before he could turn, a voice spoke. That voice was hard and yet mellow, rich and as port-winey as any post captain's had every right to be.

"Well, you young devil, Fox. Now what mischief have you been getting up to?"

CHAPTER THREE

Captain Richard Cloughton commanding His Majesty's Ship of the Line *Balthazar* stood in the doorway, his bulldog face lowering, his blunt chin thrusting aggressively, his pouched eyes fixed on Lieutenant Fox. His bulbous stomach sagged out his waistcoat and breeches. His blue coat, although new and impeccably brushed, looked rumpled. Captain Cloughton was one officer who bemoaned the loss of the white facings to captains' coats that had happened on the First of June, 1795. A damned fine way of celebrating the first anniversary of the great victory of the Glorious First of June, Captain Black Dick Cloughton had said, and burped, and his wine-red cheeks had turned scarlet then crimson and then purple, and he had coughed until the tears squeezed past his engorged eyes.

He liked his tipple, did Black Dick Cloughton.

He banged his ivory-tipped ebony cane onto Don Salvator's fine tessellated floor. The hilt of his hundred-pound presentation sword of honour swung forward with his vehemence.

"Well, you young rip? What's all this deviltry?" He waved a lace handkerchief about as though driving flies as shepherds herd sheep. "I've read your report. If you expect me to believe that—why, Mr. Fox—d'ye take me for a simpleton?"

"Indeed no, sir."

"Well then, you black imp of Satan, what have you to say for yourself, bigod?"

23

Old Black Dick Cloughton had always been like this. He roared and blustered and threatened darkly of a flogging through the Fleet; and he would do just that, too, if the occasion warranted. But Fox had served as a junior lieutenant in Captain Cloughton's *Invulnerable*, five-and-a-half years ago—a time of hectic action and surprising results, given all the circumstances—and Fox knew Cloughton, as near as anyone could, approached somewhere near the perfections of a captain required by G. A. Fox, Esqr. Cloughton was no Cuthbert Rowlands—no officer, not Troubridge, not Collingwood, not any other of the brilliant circle around Nelson—could match the excellencies of Captain Sir Cuthbert Rowlands. But if out of all the captains on the list Fox had to choose his commander, he would choose Cloughton.

Mind you—there was flap-eared chinless wonder Percy Staunton to consider now . . .

"Every word of my report is true, sir."

"The devil you say!"

"If I may say, sir, it gives me very great pleasure to see you."

"Hmph."

The way Cloughton said that silly word deprived it of all the silliness it held in the mouths of other officers.

"You took a thumping great Spanish three-decker first-rate? With a boat's crew, half a dozen marines, a gaggle of heathen Turks and—" Here Cloughton paused and swiped at the sweat streaming on his brow and scarlet cheeks, and took a visible grip on himself. "And a damned harem?"

"Yes, sir."

"A harem?" Cloughton gazed about the elegant room. "Sink me!" he exclaimed. "Young Fox, skipper of a floating brothel!"

Fox had expected this. This was the way the
24

rumours would go, the scuttlebutt, the laughter and jibes. He was aware as it were by some seventh sense creeping from his forehead and overhearing the mental processes of Cloughton's brain, just what the captain would say next. Nelson had boarded *San Nicolas* and used her as a bridge to board *San Josef* at the two-and-a-half-years-old battle of Saint Vincent. The navy called that Nelson's Patent Bridge for Boarding First Rates—Nelson's Patent Boarding Bridge, for short. Fox had guessed what the navy would call what he had done.

And now Captain Cloughton confirmed that.

"God rot me!" he cried. "Fox's Patent Boarding Brothel!"

Fox stood there. His face remained its usual gargoyle. He did not reply.

Captain Cloughton laughed until the tears squeezed out of his eyes and he coughed and spluttered and waved the hand holding the ebony cane at Fox, who brought a little gilt chair for the corpulent captain to sink into and cause to vanish from sight beneath his broad-skirted bottom. The chair creaked.

"Sink me!" wheezed Cloughton. "If that don't take the biscuit."

"It is all true, sir." Fox's tones brought Cloughton's head up like a bull facing the darts.

"Hey? I remember your ways in *Invulnerable*, Mr. Fox. Demme, I still don't know what happened to Mr. Travers-Smith. I was—taken poorly—just before we fetched port."

"Yes, sir."

Of what use to repeat the story of how Fox had safely piloted *Invulnerable* through shoals that had ripped out the bottoms of a frigate and a sloop? Cloughton, who suffered from some sinking sickness that did not take kindly to spirits, had been raving

25

then, not so much blind drunk as stricken with a maniac's illness. Fox, too, would have liked to know just what Mr. Travers-Smith had been doing then. But this was all in the past. Cloughton clearly had never known it was Fox who had saved his ship; telling him now would rightly bring instant suspicion.

"Haven't been keeping too well, as it is, just lately." Cloughton struggled to thrust a forefinger and thumb into a fob pocket against the impressive swell of his stomach. He struggled and at last, like a whaler hauling in his harpoon, brought out a silver snuffbox. He panted. Then, with due ritual he took a pinch, offered the box to Fox, who declined gracefully, and so, with many a gasp and wriggle, contrived the snuffbox back into its embrace with his belly.

"Now, Mr. Fox. They're tryin' you tomorrow for cowardice and desertion in the face of the enemy."

Incredibly—impossibly—that tidy trifle had escaped Fox in the last few moments. Now everything rushed back in on him. His face betrayed nothing.

"Yes, sir."

Cloughton thrust his stick at the tessellated paving between his feet, leaned down on it heavily, gave himself a rolling hitch of convulsive blubber, and hoisted himself out of the little gilt chair. He strode across to Fox and stood looking down. Fox could not step back, he could not take that damn-you-to-hell look he gave taller men who stared down on him. Perforce, he had to tilt his head and look up.

"Well, Mr. Fox?"

In a voice as harsh and uncompromising as the bellow of a broadside, Fox said: "The charges are not true, sir."

"Very good." Cloughton waved his stick and Fox, understanding precisely the nature of the next step, after all, he had served under this man on the quarter-

26

deck of *Invulnerable,* took himself off to the terrace where the sunshine fell with benign warmth across the shoulders of his new coat.

Rosaria greeted him with a giggle and a fluid rotation of one bare shoulder.

"Wine—Don Salvator's best Madeira, I think, Rosaria, my little chicken. The gallant captain has developed an expensive thirst at sea."

Rosaria giggled and would have back-answered; but Fox lifted a hand whose target was clearly her own delectable rear, and albeit it was all in fun, she shrieked and ran off. She came in with the wine on a chased silver tray soon enough for Cloughton and Fox to have exchanged a few generalities and cleared away a little more of the evident confusion in Cloughton's mind.

"This Captain Stone, now," said Cloughton as Fox poured the wine. He strikes me as a deuced odd fish."

Fox handed the Madeira across. He made sure he had a full glass himself.

"I fancy he bears me no goodwill, sir."

"Hmph! So I gather. The feller was positively overjoyed he'd got you in his sights. His secretary's fixed up all the damned paper-work. Deputy judge-advocate and all that rot. He's got a knife sharpening for you, young Fox."

"Yes, sir."

"Still," said Cloughton comfortably. "He's a sight junior to me. I'll sit as President." He leaned towards Fox as though about to impart great and glorious information. When he spoke Fox understood that what he was saying was, in sober truth, great and glorious—for Cloughton.

"I'm very near the top of the List, now, Mr. Fox. I'll live to fly my flag, yet, mark my words."

"My sincere congratulations, sir."

"I ain't one of your top-drawer captains," went on Cloughton, accepting another glass. "I never had the advantage of a noble lord, or of seats in the House. But I've made my way by sheer merit, yes, Mr. Fox. That's how I've done it."

Fox nodded. He knew as well as anyone else that Cloughton's Interest came from his home town where friends of the family were by way of being minor gentry and as well-heeled as any parvenue grown rich on iron and coal. They carried the Interest that had brought Cloughton his posting. From that moment his flag rank was secure, provided he lived long enough. He was also, in the cant phrase of the time, a thorough-paced Tory. Given the administration, that helped. Fox had kept scrupulously apart from declaring his politics. Maybe he ought to throw his hat in the ring and shout for the bloated Tories. Still, they might be out of office any day now, and the lean and ascetic Whigs take their place. He'd get no preferment if that happened and he was a known Tory. It was a case of roundabouts and swings.

Lady Holland was not making herself popular by her politics, and what little Fox knew of the situation, maybe the Tories would stay in office to fight Bonaparte until the war was ended. Whenever that might be.

Cloughton's sweating face loomed over Fox and he started back. The gallant captain was casting about for his cane.

"Devil take it! Had it a minute ago."

For a frightful moment Fox thought Cloughton was going to have another of his turns. The man just shouldn't drink liquor of any sort. But he did, and would continue to do so, and, consequently, would continue to foam at the mouth, and rave and fall down, and become a gibbering lunatic, from time to time.

The cane was found and another glass taken and

Don Salvator bustled in, all smiles, pleased that he had found another British captain who might become a profitable friend.

Life, so Fox saw, would go on no matter if he was found guilty and hanged at the yard-arm.

The matter of the missing witnesses brought a massive frown to the broad countenance of Captain Cloughton.

"A damned bad business, Mr. Fox. Deuced unfortunate. There is Commander Sanders' report. There is Captain Staunton's. But you must understand I ought not to discuss certain things with you at this stage, Mr. Fox. Just that there are no depositions from the men who might prove your report true without question."

Without question.

There was the rub. There would be very many questions over the report this tarpaulin lieutenant had had the effrontery to send in.

"Well, young Fox. There are five post captains to sit in judgment on you tomorrow. We know how one of 'em thinks already. As to the others—well, we shall see."

Fox wondered then if, just perhaps, Cloughton had a much better idea of how his *Invulnerable* had gone through those shoals than he admitted. Otherwise, Fox could see no reason for this crusty, bibulous, self-centcrod old sea-dog—as no doubt he liked to think of himself—caring one whit for a tearaway devil like George Abercrombie Fox.

Mind you—Cloughton might have an old score to settle with Stone. That was always possible. Many and varied were the feuds that coloured the navy and made social contacts very often like steeple-chasing where there was no knowing what obstacle might next crop up. Fox went to walk with Cloughton as the captain

29

left. Cloughton fussily adjusted his clothes, clapped his hat on firmly, gripped his cane and kerchief. He looked back at Fox and his eyes near disappeared as his cheeks swelled up, scarlet and glistening. His pendulous stomach shook.

"That's something the navy won't forget," he said. "Bigod no! Fox's Patent Boarding Brothel!"

He was still laughing and spluttering and choking as Fox turned away and went to find a rum bottle. It was all right for Cloughton and the other post captains. They weren't running the risk of finding their necks in a hempen noose, their feet dancing on air.

CHAPTER FOUR

The thought of God often occurred to Fox at times when He would seem to be absent from most sailormen's minds. Most sailors thought of God just before going into action, or when sentenced to flogging or punishments of the other kinds available under the Articles of War. Fox was well aware of what Doctor Johnson had said a prospective hanging would do to a man's powers of concentration. For his own part, he often wondered why God bothered with the kinds of men Fox came into contact with in the navy, men Fox would as lief see pitched overboard. There must be some rhyme and reason to it all, why lords and ladies possessed so much power and wealth and why so many ordinary poor men and women starved and sold themselves and died in circumstances of agony and filth and squalor.

Fox had attended enough Divine Services held aboard ship to distinguish between those that meant some trifle of religious comfort to the hands, and those that were mere charades, formal obedience to the letter of naval law. When the Articles of War were read by the captain, as was requisite, a whole new depth of meaning was injected into Divine Service. He had carried out his duties punctiliously when acting as commander of *Raccoon*. In some ships Divine Service was a mere masquerade, a farce, oftentimes an excuse for ferocious hazing of the hands.

So that for him to think of God now, when he faced

31

the prospect of hanging, drawing and quartering, seemed to him a not unnatural state of mind. Fox commended himself to his Maker, made up his mind to smash down the first sentry who tried to stop him escaping, and then went forward as a simple human being, as George Abercrombie Fox, into whatever his court martial might bring.

Rosaria walked into the room, wiggling her bottom in her usual enticing way, carrying his shoes which had been newly polished. He kicked off the alpargatas Don Salvator had loaned him and one of the rope-soled shoes flew close to Rosaria's ear, whereat she squealed.

"Ay de mi!"

An unsettling feeling of light-headedness possessed him. He almost laughed at the serving girl with her bright eyes and her voluptuous figure and her cunning little ways. He wanted to reach out and encompass the world, and at the same time he wanted to roll up into a ball and disappear.

"A hidalgo," said Rosaria. She rolled her eyes. "He is talking to the master below." She sighed suddenly, and two large and glistening tears rolled from her dark eyes.

"Estupido!" said Fox. A few moments of questioning sufficed to unravel the mystery. Rosaria was crying because Fox—que hombre!—was being taken away to have his head cut off, and the gentleman below was a naval lieutenant, a guardias, so Rosaria said, sniffing, hating the unknown lieutenant below.

"Que mujer!" said Fox. He got off the bed and advanced on Rosaria. She dropped the shoes, knowing what to expect.

"Con prisa!" she said. Fox knew she meant that he must make haste to get dressed and descend below stairs to walk forth to his doom. He chose to understand her in a different sense, which he made unmistakable by seizing her in his arms and bestowing a long and extremely passionate kiss on her full lips. Those lips were rich, pouting like crushed grapes, sweet. She fell limply against him. So the Royal Navy were going to court martial him today. So very well. But before then Fox would amuse himself in ways in which he was thoroughly expert. He showed with Rosaria on the bed just what he thought of courts martial.

Then—and only then—he condescended to get dressed.

His brand new hat could not be found.

"Dios mios!" he shouted. Rosario, still flushed, cast about the room but could find no trace of the new hat. She left at a run with her skirts flickering about those slender and provocative ankles. By the time she returned Fox was dressed in all his finery. He guessed the lieutenant below would be the Provost Marshal appointed on the occasion. No doubt Don Salvator was wondering what was keeping his guest. Had Fox received a warrant to act as Provost Marshal on an officer not in a ship he would not have waited tamely below. He'd have been up the stairs and yanked the prisoner out of bed by whatever came handy. Obvious thoughts of Rosaria made him shout and she rustled in at the door carrying his old abomination of a hat.

Her face was stricken.

The story made Fox shout and almost throw the hat to the floor and jump on it. The damage would have made little difference to it. He refrained, for Rosaria had been at his hat with a brush and an ink-bottle, and she had stitched up the wide sabre-cut far more neatly than Parson had cobbled it together. The story was that Alfredo's goat had found Fox's hat set out in the sun to dry, and had incontinently eaten it up.

33

Typical, Fox said, typical. Here he was to face a court martial for his life and guts, and a damned goat ate his brand new hat, and he was reduced to attending with his old abortion, bearing all the ravages of years at sea, pistol-ball notches and all, sabre-cuts and all. Its shape was unmentionable. With a curse Fox clapped the thing on his head, kissed Rosaria, slapped her rump, and bashed off down the stairs.

What the hell! This was the hat that had witnessed his incredible doings. What more fitting, then, that it should witness his final drama?

The Provost Marshal on the occasion turned out to be thin and elegant and icily polite. He was responsible for Lieutenant Fox's due arrival at the court martial on time.

At eight bells when the boatswain's mates would pipe for breakfast, on this morning the court martial gun would fire and the union flag would rise to the mizzen peak of *Balthazar*. By that time, although this was customarily a warning, all those persons having business at the court martial would be aboard. Fox wondered, idly at first, what the court might make of being kept waiting.

The idea intrigued him.

"Lieutenant Fox?" Tall and icy though this lieutenant was, he nevertheless looked ill at ease, an uneasiness he concealed remarkably well, so that Don Salvator had been rattling on in fine style.

"Yes."

The warrant crackled in the lieutenant's hand.

That was merely the warrant appointing him Provost Marshal on the occasion, a legal document he needed to remove Fox. The proceedings finished, Fox said to this Lieutenant Aiken—he was second in *Balthazar*— "You have my sword?"

The faintest hint of a sniff indicated what Aiken

34

thought of a five-ball sword. His own gleamed at his side, a thing of elegant beauty and regulation rectitude, modern, a naval arm based on the light cavalry sword of 1796. Unlike Fox's five-ball with its ivory grip, Aiken's weapon had a finger-ridged grip, which ran around into a brass curve replacing a real pommel. Fox considered it too heavily curved; but, undeniably, it was a useful weapon and would be used to cut him down or spit him through if he tried to run. So—this supercilious Lieutenant Aiken might be the first to feel Fox's fist in his mouth, his fingers around his throat.

These thoughts made Fox indifferent as Aiken led out. From the quays at the foot of Pigtail Steps scores of boats were dancing across the water, plying from the steps to the crowded shipping. Merchant ships of all the various types to be found trading in the Mediterranean made up the vast majority of that shipping; somewhat down towards the entrance of this magnificent anchorage lay the men-of-war. *Lynx* and *Sea Foam* were there, as Fox had seen them before. Slightly apart from them, as befitted a ship of the line, lay Captain Cloughton's *Balthazar*. Fox had said a sincere goodbye and many thankyou's to Don Salvator. He had given Rosaria a scooped handful of the gold he had taken and, as he fully intended, reserved for his men, a pittance saved from all their ferocious looting of enemy vessels. The rest had gone down with *Princessa Cristina Maria*. How he had looked forward to bringing the old *Maria* into this anchorage! She would have dwarfed everything in sight. That would have shown these snooty lords just what a simple tarpaulin lieutenant like George Abercrombie Fox could do, bigod, it would!

But—the old *Maria* had sunk. All the men who could prove what he had done, could prove he had not

35

run away, were absent. The lords would look at their reports and their papers, and look at him, and they'd condemn him. They'd condemn him.

"Captain Cloughton has sent his own barge for you, Mr. Fox."

Aiken clearly had not known what to make of that order when he had received it. Captains' barges must, of course, be occupied on many various errands and not simply be used exclusively for ferrying the captains about an anchorage; but, still and all, as Aiken clearly thought, sending the captain's barge for a prisoner facing court martial smacked of some gross dereliction of duty somewhere.

The idea of delaying his arrival and so making the court wait tickled Fox's fancy. It could easily be done; there were ways and ways to a man of Fox's malignant ingenuity. But he paused. Captain Cloughton sat as the President, it would be his court. To keep them all waiting would in a real sense demean Cloughton, make him furious. And, if Fox read the signs aright, the only slender hope he had in all this flim-flammery was Cloughton. If the crusty old bastard bore him some goodwill over the *Invulnerable* affair, it would be foolish of Fox to throw it back in the man's face— more, it would, bearing in mind his family of Foxes, be criminal.

With something of regret, then, G. A. Fox descended into the boat so as to allow Aiken to enter last.

The barge's crew were dressed with extraordinary smartness, wearing blue round-jackets, red waistcoats, wide straw hats and trousers of white with thin red stripes. Unusually smart? Fox fancied they might have tidied themselves up with extra care on the morning of a court martial; but clearly Captain Cloughton had done well for himself, and could afford to outfit his barge's crew in style.

36

The oars flashed in the sunshine, the blades dipped as one, and the boat surged ahead.

The men all wore long pigtails. This was an increasingly unfamiliar sight, and most of these queues, Fox knew, would be false. Evidently the good Cloughton was set in his ways, unwilling to change.

As the barge pulled across the water towards the seventy-four, where the union flag fluttered with so ominous a gaiety from the mizzen peak, Fox felt that weird and unsettling light-headedness afflicting him again. Perhaps it was some result of his wound. Perhaps it was that he was a trifle mad—no, everybody in the navy was mad—but a different kind of madness that expressed itself in this eerie detachment from reality.

The court would find him guilty. On the evidence to be laid before it, it could do no other, so Fox conjectured. Very well, then. He was only anxious to have it over with, so that he might bash this supercilious Lieutenant Aiken over his elegant hat and take off into a life of piracy.

But, because he was George Abercrombie Fox and would fight and struggle until the very last breath was wrung from his body, he would not escape now; but he would go to his doom, cursing them all most foully, and wait and see what happened. Then . . .

Balthazar was a fine, well-found vessel and her great aft cabin, as was to be expected, glowed and glittered with the morning sun pouring golden through her massed array of stern windows. Fox blinked. The blindingly polished table had been placed athwartships, and the five post captains sat in judgment with their backs to the light. Fox was waved to a chair to his right. An empty chair on his left waited for the first witness. Fox had sent in his list of witnesses; none was available to be called. The Deputy Judge Advocate sat

37

at the far left-hand end of the table, to starboard, surrounded by the impedimenta of his trade. Where Fox lived a life surrounded by guns and ephemerae and masts and yards, the secretary lived surrounded by papers and ink horns and sanders and the portly bound volumes of naval law.

The thought occurred to Fox that the court would not have before it the logs of *Raccoon*. They might have provided interesting reading for this mousy, fussy, drip-nosed little man.

And now a strange dream-like quality descended for Fox over the entire proceedings. Sounds reached him as though bellowed, whispering, from the far horizons. The light daggered into his eyes. They adjusted slowly. Now he could make out the massive form of Cloughton in the centre, leaning forward, clearing away the very necessary preliminaries demanded by the regulations. To his right, which meant the captain was the next senior, sat Captain Hyatt, a mahogany-faced individual with the mournful expression of a pressed-man. How he would regard a jumped-up lieutenant, Fox had no need to surmise. He wore a gold medal on a ribbon around his neck, as did Cloughton. To Cloughton's left as next senior captain sat Captain Lanchester of *Sea Foam*. Fox wondered, fleetingly, how he was progressing in his seduction of Mrs. Pratt.

Then—to the right of Hyatt sat Captain Lemuel Stone.

The man sat hunched, brooding, not looking at Fox. For Fox himself the idea of a rat caught in a trap, with a terrier leering upon him, jumped with frightful clarity into his mind.

Stone and Lanchester, at the least, must have gone drinking together. Stone would have worked well, insinuation, innuendo, calumny. Most of them true, of course, Fox conceded, and all the more damaging for that. Stone would not rest until he had paid Fox back a hundredfold.

The first post captain sat at the extreme left, flanking Lanchester, a small, intense man with lips that had at one time received a sword-cut so that he wore the look of a man with a hare-lip. His eyes stared straight at Fox for a long time, as though the captain was weighing up this tarpaulin lieutenant against a life-time of sea experience. When Mr. Parkinson, the Deputy Judge Advocate, read out the list of the captains' names preparatory to administering the oath, Fox learned the last post captain was a Captain Falconer. The coincidence of the name made Fox that little more determined. He was no tame rabbit to be plucked into the air by a Falcon. Cloughton then administered the oath to Parkinson who read the charge.

At this point the witnesses should have left the court.

Fox had no witnesses to call, although his list lay on the table before Cloughton. Surprisingly, Cloughton called all their names, interrogating Parkinson each time, to be answered with the dry response that they were not at the moment in court.

Against Fox no witnesses were brought, for those of any consequence were at sea with Commander Sanders. Fox wondered if this might in some way count as an irregular proceeding, and if he might not be able to appeal on the grounds of some technicality. Parkinson soon brought that idea to a head and lanced it; all the proofs required lay on the table. There were Commander Sanders' report, his sworn statement, the depositions of those members of the crew of *Raccoon* he had taken with him, and the minutes of his court martial. On these written records alone Fox would be judged.

Legal or not, it would stick once the judgment was made. My Lords of the Admiralty were loath to overturn the findings of a court, for that smacked of an assault on the sacred edifice of discipline and authority.

The Deputy Judge Advocate hummed and hawed, swallowed, worked a finger under his neck cloth, and then began to read out Fox's report. He called Fox 'The Prisoner.'

The summary of evidence on the table related only to Fox's alleged desertion during the time *Raccoon* had been run aground, the attack of the French, Sanders' departure in the French open boat. Everything after that in Fox's report had nothing either for it or against it. However, Parkinson read it all out—the search to the north for water, the capture of the lateener, Fox's escape into Tuscany and his miraculous rescue of his men at Cavallo. Naturally—very naturally!—Fox had made no mention of his reasons for all this, his greedy search for the Treasure of the Cavallo, the treasure bequeathed to him by Captain Louis Lebonnet, of his reluctant relinquishment of that fabulous treasure, looted by the Vieux Moustaches of Bonaparte from Italian churches, to Maria and her Popish friends.

The report covered his subsequent taking of the privateer brig *Clothilde,* her sinking after the rescue of the Turks and that damned harem—how Fox was aware of the raised eyebrows here, the looks cast in his direction, the hands raised to mouths—of their landing on the island and their capture of the Spanish three-decker one hundred and twelve *Princessa Cristina Maria.*

Here Captain Stone interrupted.

"And do you expect us to believe this nonsense?"

Before Fox could speak, Cloughton ruled that the report must be finished, and Parkinson continued. But Stone sat back in his chair, contemptuously, ostenta-

40

tiously playing with his pen, flicking the feathers with an irritating fluttering.

The three-deckers's rescue of Captain Percy Staunton and his crew when his frigate, *Pylas,* sank under the onslaught of a pack of Spanish gunboats and the subsequent burning and loss of the old *Maria* were read out.

Cloughton turned his pouched eyes on Parkinson.

"Ought we not to have the minutes of Captain Staunton's court martial before us?"

Parkinson shuffled his papers. "They have been forwarded to Gibraltar, sir, under orders."

Fox saw that, all right. At least, it could be proved in court that he *had* brought a captured Spanish three-decker to the aid of Captain Staunton. Just where he got her, though, would remain in doubt. Did they think he'd picked her up cheap in a side-alley in Cadiz, for God's sake?

Stone said: "We are here to try the prisoner for cowardice and desertion in the face of the enemy. I think Commander Sanders' report covers that adequately."

And sod you too, said Fox to himself.

Stone would concentrate on that end of the story. Cloughton's attempt to introduce what Fox had done subsequently, a story that ought to refute the charges absolutely, must fail if put to the test without a single witness. Cloughton had made attempts to have the trial postponed so that Fox's witnesses might be procured; but the machinery had been in motion. Now Fox sensed the animosity between Stone and Cloughton. There *was* something there, bigod . . .

Captain Falconer who spoke with something of an impediment by reason of his mangled mouth, said: "And you took a first-rate with a boat's crew, a few Turks—and a harem?"

41

"Yes, sir."

"I'd dearly like to hear how that was done—"

Cloughton coughed and spluttered and Fox knew what the old wretch was thinking. Fox himself tended to disguise the horrid branding name under the initials "F.P.B.B." but the sting still remained.

Captain Stone said something in a voice low enough for Fox to miss. Automatically he turned to look at the gross body that housed still the same toadying brain that had given him so much refined torture, and he could not see. The light from the stern windows dimmed and blurred. That infernal ring of purple and black was creeping around his left eye. He reached up and rubbed it, as always uselessly, and then let his hand return to his side in a casual movement. If these post captains for one moment suspected they had a purblind lieutenant to deal with he'd be on the beach and starving before he could say Davy Jones.

He knew what Captain Falconer meant. In the jargon of naval reports—a jargon Fox had fully employed to cloak what had really happened—the incident of the girls enticing the Spanish soldiers and seamen whilst Fox and his men rowed like maniacs for the three-decker had been neatly glossed over in a cant phrase. Falconer looked a likely sort. That maiming of his lips might not have turned him sour.

As the proceedings unwound their painful way a slight pause ensued in which, now almost unable to see a blind thing, Fox heard Lieutenant Aiken at his side cough and shift uncomfortably. As he resumed his poker-stiff presence the sound of a quill racing desperately across paper, squealing and spluttering, told Fox that Cloughton was waiting for Parkinson to catch up with his note-taking.

Now Fox could see nothing at all. His right eye had joined his left. Blackness absolute encompassed him.

He sat there, knowing his face betrayed nothing of his handicap, his eyes with their Arctic ice-floe damn-you-to-hell look—as, among others, this same Lemuel Stone had once said of them—open and piercing. He listened avidly. If he had to rise now and walk he'd have to do so purely on the basis of his understanding of ships and his memory of the geography of this great cabin, finding his way over the black and yellow painted canvas squares.

A question was being put to him by Lanchester.

"What reason do you give for not reporting to your captain after *Raccoon* grounded?"

It was in the report; but they wanted him to condemn himself out of his own mouth. Lanchester, probably, was tied up with Stone.

"A body of French soldiers attacked us, sir. I led a party up the beach to drive them off."

He remembered that, he remembered the mad run, plunging and lunging in the sand and gravel, the muskets hammering, the bayonets and the swords bloody-red, Phillips, dying as he watched.

G. A. Fox essayed a prod.

"I led a successful attack against the French soldiers and drove them off the ridge. When I returned to the wreck of *Raccoon* Commander Sanders had left in a French boat—"

Before he could go on, Stone's voice broke in: "We have only your word for that!"

"Yes," said Lanchester. "There is no proof."

Cloughton grunted and wheezed—Fox could imagine those bloated scarlet cheeks glistening, that rotund belly quivering—and got out: "I think the court understands, Captain Lanchester, that you mean to imply the proof has not yet been brought into evidence."

"It's clear enough, surely, sir?"

"Are you getting all this down, Mr. Parkinson?"

"As fast as I can, sir."

"Steady as you go, then."

Fox wanted to believe he would be found not guilty —no-one was ever innocent in the navy—but despite his growing awareness of the animosity between Stone and Cloughton, from the way the unsupported testimony went he knew he must face up to his declared intention of knocking down his guards, of diving overboard and of turning pirate.

But he was blind!

How could he even escape if he couldn't see where to strike?

He was fully aware that Lieutenant Aiken, the Provost Marshal, would cut him down the instant he essayed an escape. Aiken had that thin and homicidally-dedicated look about him. The pain in his eyes meant nothing; he'd stand ten times that pain if only he could see again!

The case was plain. Stone and Lanchester between them could persuade the taciturn Captain Hyatt to their way of thinking. Falconer might waver. Cloughton would be left out on a limb, always assuming he cared a single jot or tittle for Lieutenant Fox. It was all over, then. The verdict would be guilty. Then, when he was told to stand up, he'd turn and fall over something and sprawl on his face and they'd take him up and hang him up and after that they'd deal with his entrails.

It had to be all over for George Abercrombie Fox.

A buzz of disregarded conversation about him was ripped through by a voice—a voice he knew, saying: "Aye aye, sir."

CHAPTER FIVE

In his agonising blindness Fox turned to look back and saw nothing; but he heard voices more beautiful than a heavenly choir. He heard the sound of men's feet on the black and yellow squares, the clearing of a throat, the shuffling of bodies.

Parkinson was swearing in a witness.

"You are John Carker, Master's Mate of His Britannic Majesty's frigate *Furieuse?*"

"I am."

"Ah, Mr. Carker," said Cloughton. "Yes or no, if you please."

"Aye aye, sir."

"You were formerly," went on Parkinson, "Master's Mate of His Britannic Majesty's late sloop of war *Raccoon?*"

"Yes."

Fox just sat there.

Carker!

The good Carker, risen like Aphrodite from the sea, come bearing succour and aid!

Impossible.

Percy Staunton had taken *Furieuse* on duty that should have kept him at sea for many weeks yet. So— how could the frigate have returned to Mahon? Had there been an action? Prizes? Perhaps—and here Fox's heart gave a most infernal jump—perhaps there had been casualties and some of his hands had been killed. He fretted over those hands of his, he, G. A. Fox, the toughest bastard in the navy, the man who cared for no one and expected no-one to care for him. Suppose young Ben Ferris had been killed, or Barnabas, or Wilson, or Slattery? He couldn't bear the thought of losing Joachim, his German gunner's mate, or of Parsons, his servant. And—what of that young limb of Satan, Mr. Midshipman Lionel Grey?

He forced himself to listen as Carker soberly related what had happened. Carker's version exactly paralleled his own. Well, it would, as Carker had seen what Fox wanted him to see, had been fed with all the right words and sentences. That it was as near the truth as, in this court, to make no difference, helped.

Then—blessedly then!—Grey was sitting in the witness chair and running again over the events from his point of view.

A glimmer of light trickled in under Fox's right eye. He blinked. He could make out the series of oblongs of light from the enormous stern windows. They brightened. A row of black blobs punctured them— the heads of the five post captains. He waited as Grey went on talking, quietly, evenly, his perfectly modulated voice, so refined when necessary, giving exactly the right tone to what he was saying. He finished as Fox's sight came fully back: "And I must say that I have never seen a more gallant action in my life than that of Mr. Fox. But for him the whole crew would have perished."

Fox had been nearly out. Like a prize-fighter on the South Downs he had been on the ground, bloody and bruised, vainly struggling to stand up. And now—his first evil look flashed to where Stone sat. Stone's face had paled, and he was ripping the barbs from the feather of his pen. Then—and only then—did Fox permit himself the unbridled luxury of looking at Mr. Midshipman Lionel Grey.

Grey looked wonderful.

The mid was no longer a boy—he had never really been a boy from the moment he had first reported aboard *Raccoon*—but this time of absence had given Fox a fresh view of him, so that he saw that Grey was, indeed, a man. He was twenty. He'd be a lieutenant at any time now, and then—and then he'd be posted inside a year. Fox had tried to hold a rancour against the lad for that, and did, too, bigod! But the rancour was a mere nothing compared with the hatred he felt for jumped-up nincompoops like Stone and Beckworth, who was now Lord Lymm.

After that it was a procession. Even Hogan, the carpenter, who at the beginning of their mad escapade had not been one of Fox's men, could not sing Mr. Fox's praises high enough. Joachim in his thick but adequate English related in technical detail the luscious professional tricks of Mr. Fox, and the catapult with which they had blown up a boom and burned a French corvette. Barnabas followed and here Fox felt a strangeness about the big and burly red-haired man, a constraint. But Barnabas related his version, and did not dwell at all on his own functions as acting boatswain. Fox was aware that a mystery surrounded Barny Barnabas; and now he guessed the tough seaman had ventured into the courtroom with great trepidation.

But—he had done so, in order to tell the court of the crazily gallant things that Fox had done.

Then came Josephs, stroke oar when he had had his own boat.

Captain Stone interrupted.

"Surely we have heard enough? These men have been well primed. They all tell the same story. They have it off pat."

Fox looked at Cloughton. The blubber heaved as

47

Cloughton settled his belly more comfortably. Fox saw that Cloughton was enjoying this.

"I believe it is relevant to have all the facts we can have, Captain Stone."

Falconer said: "I would like to ask the marine sergeant—" He consulted his notes. "Sergeant Cartwright, called next. He was with the Turkish women."

You randy old devil! said Fox to himself. Still, with that dreadful wound mangling his lips, perhaps Falconer couldn't bring a pretty girl to kiss him these days.

Cartwright, impeccable in brilliant scarlet, very formal, gave his evidence in a bellow that Cloughton vainly tried to bring down in scale from a parade ground order to a quarterdeck order. Cartwright spoke his piece—Falconer the while listening with a contortion of his lips that might have been a smile.

By the time Halliwell and Wilson had given their evidence, Captain Lemuel Stone had had enough.

He slammed down the remnants of his pen.

"I submit this is all unnecessary! We are here to try the prisoner for desertion on the beach of Santa Clara—"

Fox said: "With respect, sir. We rounded Santa Clara in the storm. Commander Sanders and Mr. Macbridge piled her up on Santa Anna."

The silence hung.

Fox had deliberately risked a rebuff; perhaps he had pushed too much. But bitter memories had gushed up.

"Santa Anna or Santa Clara," said Stone with a viciousness Fox sensed was not entirely, this time, for him. "You deserted on the beach, as we know from Commander Sanders' report, and the rest of this wildgoose tale is immaterial."

Captain Hyatt roused himself.

"I agree with Captain Stone. What happened on the beach is the nub of the question."

Cloughton, about to speak, caught Falconer's eye, one along from Lanchester. "I submit, sir, with due respect, that what we have heard bears materially on the charge brought against the prisoner of cowardice. I do not think a coward could have done what the prisoner has done."

"That may be so, sir!" shouted Stone. "But what of the desertion? D'you disregard what Commander Sanders says?"

"There might well have been a misunderstanding on the beach, sir."

"Misunderstanding! The prisoner and these ruffians of his seized the opportunity to run off and bumped into a small patrol of French—"

Fox could see that Stone believed this himself. Captain Lanchester nodded; but he kept his eyelids lowered and he looked at the papers before him on the table.

Hyatt said: "If there was a misunderstanding, I cannot see why Commander Sanders or the prisoner should have made it. It was the Commander's position and responsibility to order an attack on the French. Having done so he could not have sailed away without the men making the attack. But he did. Therefore he could not have ordered it."

Neat, considered Fox—and damned true—but it rebounded against him, not against wonder-boy Sanders.

He was nowhere safely clawed off this lee shore yet.

"Commander Sanders," Stone was saying, his face now as red and glistening as Cloughton's own, "is a gallant officer and an ornament to the profession."

Cloughton took out his kerchief, wrapped his face in it, blew like an eleven-gun salute, and flourished the white lace around a few times before stowing it back in his tail pocket.

Fox's face remained graven. But he said to himself: "Good old Black Dick Cloughton! So much for Commander bloody Richard bloody Sanders!"

"I did not think we were here to question the competence of Commander Sanders—" began Cloughton.

Stone clearly had been goaded by reasons beyond Fox's fathoming. Now Captain Stone half-turned so that he bent to glare past Captain Hyatt. "The truth is, Captain Cloughton, you have never forgiven Commander Sanders for taking the swab and the command of *Raccoon* you had thought should go to your friend Captain Laker's son!"

The charge in outright public domain like this might be unusual; but unusual circumstances had dragged it forth. Fox expected Cloughton to explode. Instead, with his cheeks glistening scarlet and bulging with veins, his mad eyes glaring, Cloughton placed both hands palm down on the table, forced his gross bulk back in the chair, and visibly composed himself.

Then, speaking like a fine Spanish rapier slipping in between the ribs, he said: "I was unaware that my friendship for Captain Laker, or his son, constituted a breach of the regulations. I remember, Captain Stone, that I congratulated you at the time that your own nephew, Commander Sanders, had received his command."

Silence.

Well, of course . . .

Those, Fox surmised, were the thoughts jostling in everyone's brain.

The old devil, Interest, at work again . . .

No wonder Stone had been so violently against Fox even without the animus of those old days in *Nico-*

demus to spur him on. If Fox was adjudged not guilty, then where did that leave Sanders?

Right in it, up to his neck, considered Fox, and the best of British luck to him.

Hyatt looked up quickly and his elbow knocked an ink horn spinning. The blue-black splash stained all across the glistening table. Somehow, it looked dark and ominous there.

In a gale you clamped the ink horns closed. Parkinson, who had been scribbling away with desperate haste, squealed and leaped clear as the inky stream dripped over the edge of the table. He, like anyone else, did not want inkstains on his white breeches. Still, Fox thought, that was a hazard of his profession just as dodging roundshot was a hazard of Fox's own.

Fox could not fail to be aware that Cloughton had allowed the court martial to degenerate into a farce; but he sensed that the cunning old bastard knew exactly what he was doing. He had wanted all this damning evidence about Stone in the record. No one would blink at what Stone had done—although Fox thought that had he known in those days when Sanders came aboard *Raccoon* so cockily to take command he might have dotted Stone's eye for him had they met—but they most certainly did not want the powers of Interest so flaunted. Stone had dropped an almighty black mark onto his record, and Black Dick Cloughton was chortling away, and gasping and choking with merriment.

Sod 'em all! Just so long as George Abercrombie Fox got off, and could go back to earning a dishonest penny, then all would be well.

The verdict did not take long. It was clear enough to Fox what had happened: Lanchester had stuck loyally by Stone and given a guilty verdict. Cloughton and Falconer had openly shown they believed Fox,

51

and Hyatt had swayed with the wind—as well as the evidence, although that mattered little when feuds broke into open conflict.

The spilled ink having been cleaned up, the Deputy Judge Advocate could resume his place. Everyone stilled.

Captain Black Dick Cloughton made it short and sweet.

"This court finds you not guilty of the charges preferred. In addition we compliment you on your subsequent conduct. You are free."

CHAPTER SIX

Mind you, he missed the excuse to bash Lieutenant Aiken over the head.

How glorious the sunshine! How sweet the breeze!

He had been freed to risk his neck once again, to run the chance of having his entrails spilled out by grape or his skull cleft by a cutlass, his head knocked off by a roundshot; but how infinitely superior those risks than being mewed up between stone walls and iron bars or of dangling at the end of the yard-arm!

Free!

"Congratulations, sir," said John Carker, his honest face one great beam of pleasure.

"Congratulations, sir," said Lionel Grey. He looked pleased, too, even if that sly little chuckle of amusement at this quaint old shellback persisted, as it always seemed to in moments of emotion.

Fox shook both their hands, solemnly. He had been given back his sword. He clapped his hat on his head. Grey's eyebrows rose.

Mr. Midshipman Grey and this confounded hat of Fox's!

"Mr. Grey, you'll be interested to hear that a goat ate that fine new hat."

"A—goat, sir?"

They stood on the gangway above the ladder waiting for *Furieuse's* boat. They had to wait until the post captains' barges had been called and the boatswain's mates had piped the side and with due solemnity

Captains Hyatt, Lanchester, Stone and Falconer had left.

Fox had had a brief word with Cloughton. He had ventured to thank Cloughton, tactfully, and Black Dick had waved him away with: "If you get up to any more larks and get into another scrape, you imp of hell, don't expect me to come a-running."

"No, sir."

"I remember you in *Invulnerable*, Mr. Fox. A right black bastard, but an officer who got things done." Cloughton had looked around, and waved his kerchief, and leaned confidentially close. "Mr. Aiken treat you civilly?"

"Very, sir."

"Ha harrum." Again that confidential scanning of the horizons bounded by his own cabin. Then: "Tell me, Mr. Fox. This Captain Staunton. D'you know him well?"

"No, sir. He has asked for me as his first—"

"Dammit, young Fox, I know that! The feller ain't a fool, then. He's nephew to Admiral Staunton, ain't he?"

"Yes, sir."

"He's put up both swabs now."

That meant Percy Staunton had completed three years as a post captain. Fox wasn't clear how he had managed to do that; but, evidently, the gods of the sea had smiled on him.

Cloughton had hummed and hawed, and then shaken hands, and finished with: "I'll no doubt be hearing from you, then, young Fox."

Normally as quick as any man on the uptake, Fox was fogged.

"I shall take that as a privilege, sir. And, once again, thank you."

"Now clear off. And, you imp of Satan, take my

54

advice. Keep away from women. Stick to rum. You can't go wrong with rum." And Cloughton had coughed and spluttered and choked until the scarlet of his face threatened to explode in gory tatters around his splendid cabin.

Now as he stood waiting for Captain Percy Staunton's barge to fetch him aboard his new domain, Fox heard Carker repeat, his honest face perplexed: "A goat, sir?"

"Aye, Mr. Carker, a goat. If I get another new hat, Mr. Carker—" And then he hauled himself up. He had been about to say that he hoped Carker would take care of it as he had of the five-ball sword. He had been meaning to cheer the good Carker. But Carker would take it so seriously, that, one day, in the heat of action more than likely, he might imperil his life just for the sake of a stupid brand new hat of Fox's.

Instead, he said what he should have said at first.

"Thank you, Mr. Carker. Thank you, Mr. Grey." Then, unlike the old Fox, like the new soft-centred Fox, he added: "The pair of you—and the hands— saved my bacon then."

With that, mercifully, *Furieuse's* boat hooked on and the bellow informing them of the fact floated up and he could go down into her without having to look again at the faces of Grey and Carker.

Not only because he was interested in Ben Ferris but, at this moment, more for the sake of saying something that would bring everything back on an even keel, Fox said to Carker: "Is Ben keeping up well with his schooling, Mr. Carker?"

"Aye, sir, he is. He's a smart lad."

"I am gratified to hear it. I have hopes for that imp, Mr. Carker. I am obliged to you."

Fox could remember with a poignant clarity the days when he had been schooled under the tuition of

Captain Cuthbert Rowlands as he had been then. At least, Ben Ferris had the advantage that he could read and write already. Merely because Fox had risked his neck and the necks of his boat's crew in rescuing Ben Ferris in that wicked gale at Palermo could not wholly explain the feelings he had for the boy. As a confirmed heterosexual—as Rosaria could testify— Fox acknowledged this weakness of his for looking out for the well-being of ship's boys. Ben was old enough to be rated A.B. now and, as soon as Fox could contrive it and Ben had mastered enough of the rudiments required, Fox was going to have him entered as a Volunteer. Then the cockpit lay open to him, and the quarterdeck. Perhaps the sight of Ben Ferris's mother dying on the beach at Palermo had something to do with it, too.

Mind you, it was damnably difficult for a youngster to concentrate on schooling on the lower deck, exposed as he was to the mockery and rough-and-tumble of the hands. But Ben Ferris had the grit, Fox knew, and he would persevere.

He might one day hoist his own flag, an Admiral of England.

It was a sobering thought.

Now he was once again in the open air, a free man —or as free as an officer in the Royal Navy who was not a post captain could ever be free—he could look about and savour the sights and sounds. The sun sprinkled the water with careless gold—a thought Fox had no wish to dwell on at the moment, considering all the gold he had so recently lost—and the idea of anyone being careless with money appalled him. *Sea Foam* and *Lynx* still lay moored close together. A little astern of them lay another frigate. This vessel Fox scrutinised with his habitual intolerance as they approached.

By God! She looked a mess!

Just what the people ashore were saying about her he had no wish to dwell on. Her yards were almost squared off—which was tantamount to saying they were cock-a-bill, in an unholy mess. He could see a rope's end dangling over her fore chains. Some of her paintwork looked as though the brush that applied it had been bereft of bristles. Still, much of a ship's paint depended on how much money her captain could afford to spend on her.

Still, Captain Percy Staunton, the favourite nephew of Admiral Staunton, should have a deep purse. If Fox was to be first lieutenant in *Furieuse*, he'd have Staunton dipping deep before the day was out.

A little gold spread carefully ashore in the yard— bribery it never was—would secure capital supplies of paint. He'd go over her with a fine tooth comb, as the saying was. He'd know every single inch of her. Already as always and as ever, George Abercrombie Fox was in love again, in love with his new ship.

He admired her lines, fine and free yet bold, with a sheer delight that sent a little shudder of anticipation through him. The loft of her masts indicated she was sparred for canvas and the rake of those masts . . . h'mm . . . Fox tilted his head as they pulled towards the frigate. He'd have her sailing with every setting known to the ingenious mind of the sailor man, and he'd sweat the crew shifting ballast until he had her running as sweet and true as she could.

Abruptly, he became aware of Grey and Carker in the sternsheets staring at him. His face congealed and they hastily looked overside. The coxswain, a robust man with a curly-head of hair and a straw hat he wore tilted so outrageously over one eye it was a marvel the hat did not fall into the boat's wake, steered well enough even for Fox as they swung up to the accommodation ladder.

Of course, there was no need for the bowman to hold up any four fingers; and his habitual "Aye, aye," signified little when the dullest eye aboard could pick out Fox's uniform.

He went up the ladder first. One day—God willing —when he went up like this he'd step on deck to the thrilling of the bosun's mates' pipes, and the crash as the marines presented arms, and the swish as the officers removed their hats.

As it was he saluted the quarterdeck and moved aft and there was Captain Percy Staunton, ears flapping, Adam's apple rising and falling like a lighter in a cross-sea, beaming and striding forward with outstretched hand.

"My dear Mr. Fox! Lay me horizontal if it ain't deucedly good to see you! 'Pon my word! I never doubted the outcome of the trial, sir, never doubted it an instant."

"Thank you, sir."

"Come below, Mr. Fox, come below. I've a tolerably good Madeira I would value your opinion of."

"That is most kind of you, sir." Fox fixed the affable nincompoop with what he knew was called his gimlet eye. Staunton swallowed and blinked. "May I take it, sir, that, as we discussed you are doing me the honour of taking me as your first?"

"Of course, Mr. Fox! Devil take it if I meant anything else! Fellers I have now—" He shut himself up, then, and repeated his demand that Fox should pray step below.

"In a moment, sir."

Fox went forward to the quarterdeck rail. It felt good—hell, it felt marvellous—thus to stand on a quarterdeck again and stare forward past the masts

58

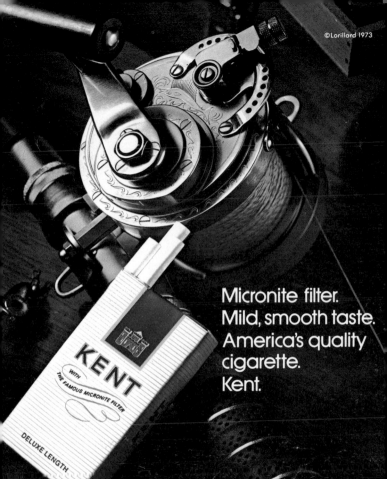

©Lorillard 1973

Micronite filter.
Mild, smooth taste.
America's quality
cigarette.
Kent.

King Size or Deluxe 100's.

Kings: 16 mg. "tar," 1.0 mg. nicotine; 100's: 19 mg. "tar," 1.2 mg. nicotine;
Menthol: 18 mg. "tar," 1.3 mg. nicotine, av. per cigarette, FTC Report Sept. '73.

Try the crisp, clean taste of Kent Menthol.

The only Menthol with the famous Micronite filter.

and the shadows of the rigging and the familiar and yet new-to-him deck of a ship once more. He let out a bellow of so ferocious a savagery that a sailor dropped his marline spike on the deck and a ship's boy wet himself.

"Get that loose end inboard forrard there! Step lively or I'll have you triced at the gangway! Bosun!"

Where the boatswain sprang from Fox didn't know; but in seconds the boatswain stood knuckling his forehead.

"Bosun. Have you inspected the set of the yards this morning?"

"Aye, sir."

Fox could go one of two ways. He could jolly the man along, be nice to him, even make a joke of it, get him to do his job properly with the velvet glove. Or he could rave and threaten and talk of disratings and floggings with the iron hand.

Fox said: "Row around the ship again, Bosun, and see the yards are squared off. I shall be on deck again and I shall inspect them myself. If they are not exactly squared off there will be changes. You will suffer, Bosun, I promise you that. Now, jump to it!"

"Aye aye, sir."

The boatswain took himself off. Fox waited a moment, letting that flat and unholy glare from his eyes travel around the deck, seeing men bending immediately to their tasks, the bosun's mate swishing their starters, the sudden hectic activity that boiled as his gaze travelled around. He waited, then he drew himself upright, turned, and stalked aft.

Captain Staunton waited for him in his cabin.

The place was elegant, with much furniture, many pictures, a liquor cupboard crammed to overflowing, painted canvas on the floor, the gleam and shine of expensive silver; in short, Fox walked into the cabin

59

of an officer with Interest, with money and with expectations.

"Try a glass of this sherry wine, Mr. Fox, and give me your opinion, sir."

Fox drank. It wasn't rum. But he knew about wines.

"It is well enough, sir, if you will forgive me for being so frank. Some rascally vintner shouted it up to you, did he?"

"Why, Mr. Fox." Percy Staunton was taken aback.

"I'll have a word with the ship's suppliers, sir. If there's money to be thrown away, we'll throw it away on the ship. We need paint, sir—" He went into a deliberately confusing technical list of his requirements that left Staunton floundering. Staunton took a long swallow, waved a limp hand, and said: "I'll leave all that to you, Mr. Fox. I only came to sea to please uncle."

"I'd best see the officers, now, sir—"

But Percy Staunton would have none of that. "All in good time, Mr. Fox, all in good time."

There was no use bottling up his question any longer, and Fox had hung onto it as long as he cared to. He took the next proffered glass, and sipped, and said: "I understood you were not due back for some time. I wondered how it is that you came back to Mahon at this time."

"Lay me horizontal, Mr. Fox. Didn't we nearly founder? I ask you, didn't we nearly turn beams end over? I can't understand it. I lost me fore and main topmasts, sir, fore and main topmasts, all gone, in a twinkling, six bells of the middle watch. We're outfitted again; but it was Port Mahon for us, Mr. Fox." He shook his head. "A sound man had the deck at the time, Mr. Fox. Deuced queer business."

"I dislike losing a spar intensely; but no sailorman can guarantee never to lose one. Even Admiral Nelson lost his at a vital moment—as Boney was thankful for."

"Ah—quite so."

"How are we mustered, sir?"

Staunton looked a trifle less vague. Any naval officer tended to concentrate his thoughts when thinking of manning his vessel. "I brought sixty from poor old *Pylas*. There were fifty waiting from various sources. And those from *Lancebrook* that went aground and broke up off Cape Dartuch. Poor Lascelles Knightly lost his life there, drowned, I'm sad to say." Percy Staunton poured more wine. "Still, we picked up most of his crew."

Now Fox knew well enough that Staunton did not mean that he and *Furieuse* had picked up the men from the sea as their vessel broke up and foundered. When your uncle was an admiral he would naturally see to it that you received the men you needed for your fine, spanking frigate when a ship's company thus came, as it were, on the market. Maybe, Fox brightened, maybe he wouldn't have to go on the business of press-ganging any more.

"With yours, Mr. Fox, that means we have two hundred and sixty—"

Fox quelled the wild elation that flashed through him.

That was as near as made no matter a full complement. There were precious few vessels afloat with their full complements. He rubbed his hands together, and Staunton, who did not mistake the gesture, nevertheless hospitably took it as a sign and rapidly poured another glass of wine for his new first lieutenant.

"Two hundred and sixty," said Fox. "Bigod, if I don't make this ship the smartest in the Fleet my name's not G. A. Fox!"

"I'll drink to that, Mr. Fox!"

"I take it the Widows' Men are accounted for?"

61

"Oh, capitally, Mr. Fox, capitally. They're all written up full and proper. You must speak to the Purser—"

"Yes, sir. Perhaps I'd best see the officers, now."

So, thus brought around to his own desires, by Staunton's words, Fox could break off this asinine although golden conversation, and take himself off to see the officers he must impress with his own authority and severity and general bloody-mindedness.

At a mooring like this no commissioned officers would stand a watch, instead the Master's Mates stood anchor watch, and there was Carker, waiting on the quarterdeck. With him was Grey.

How easy it would be to smile at them and ask them to give him the information he must have about their fellow officers! Smiling was always a painful business for Fox—well, almost always—and he had been in the position previously of asking for this kind of information. Fox, being Foxey, had other ways.

"I hear you lost some top timber, Mr. Carker."

"Aye, sir."

"Were you on deck at the time?"

"Yes, sir."

"I am surprised, Mr. Carker."

Grey coughed and scuffed his foot, then, in that damn-you cut-glass voice of his, he said: "I was on deck, as well, sir. It just happened, a freak of the wind. Some of the old Raccoons were also on deck. The officer of the watch was Mr. Haining."

"And he said—apart from the cursing—?"

Neither Carker nor Grey smiled. "He could not understand how it happened, either, sir."

"Very good. I'll speak to the officers now, the captain will be on deck shortly. Oh, and, Mr. Carker, Mr. Grey. If you lose your fore and main topmasts when I am first lieutenant I shall want to know how it happened. I shall be very interested to know how it happened." He paused. Hell! He was getting as soft as cheap butter. But, soft as butter Fox added: "Although I doubt I shall be as pleased."

"Aye aye, sir!" said Carker, and "Aye aye, sir!" said Grey.

So he was right, and the damned blackguards knew he knew. They'd smashed up Crown property, ripped the topmasts out of a spanking fine frigate, just so they could turn her around and head back to Minorca! And why should they do that? So they could give evidence at his trial. They'd planned it. It had been done with nods and winks with his men. He felt suddenly gratified that he hadn't asked who was on the wheel. Ben Ferris, or Barnabas, most likely. They could jibe her, set her aback, acting in concert with the other old Raccoons they could have the sticks out of her in a twinkling. He wondered they'd stopped at a pair of topmasts. Mutiny! That was what it had been, bigod! Mutiny, devised and put into practice on his behalf.

But—they were his men.

And—he daren't have that bruited around too much aboard or else there would be dark talk of first lieutenant's favourites, and sullen faces, and mistakes, and he'd have a hell ship on his hands. The first had to tread a tightrope of delicacy in dealing with the men. Although they might be driven like animals with colts and triced up and flogged, and hanged if need be, they were men with perhaps the quickest sense of injustice according to their own rules as any body of men anywhere.

Captain Staunton came on deck, word was passed, and presently the officers mustered back in the great aft cabin.

Without a word being said, Fox received the full impact of the hostility to him. There was hatred here.

63

These men resented his arrival. They detested and despised him.

Well, that was nothing new.

Fox would deal with them. If they did not obey his orders he'd break them, and think them well rid of.

Mr. Haining, who was now the second and who had, for a time, been acting as the first, shook hands with a bad grace.

"Glad to have you aboard, sir."

Fox turned from him with a word to the second—who was now the third—knowing how Haining lied in his teeth. He'd come from *Lancebrook* and had cherished notions. Mr. Haining was a tall and thin individual, with very black hair and eyes that darted and swerved in their sockets, with a lobe missing from his left ear, no doubt as a result of a cutlass slash or a whore's razor.

The ship's officers were gathered here: the Master, Mr. Burlington, with greying hair and a paunch; Mr. Gyver, the Purser, growing rich on his two ounces a pound; the marine lieutenant, Mr. Smythe, boney and punctilious and—a trifle shy? Fox pondered that, watching the marine in his brave scarlet. If so, it would be most unusual.

Mr. Morgan, the third, and Mr. Dillon, the fourth, completed the round up of officers of wardroom rank. There was—unfortunately to Fox—no Surgeon, and —fortunately, as far as Fox was concerned—no Chaplain.

He was aware that Staunton was making something of a show in thus trotting out his new first lieutenant in his own cabin, and having his servant pass around drinks, and generally behaving as though this was a party. Fox promised himself to make a few penetrating if casual-seeming enquiries when he got himself down into the gunroom. He took this advantage of appraising

64

his new shipmates, and trying to read something of their character from their mannerisms and spoken words, for he remained chillingly aware of the hostility towards him.

Staunton spoke quietly to him for a few moments.

"D'ye see, Mr. Fox. Dear old uncle wanted me to take a fine dashing young lieutenant he'd cut out for me from under Nelson's nose as me first. But I wasn't having any of it. Oh, dear me, no. Young Josiah can have him, says I. And there's a rip for you." Staunton drank, chuckling, his Adam's apple bobbing. He looked completely artless, a trifle sweaty, red-faced, goggle-eyed, absolutely naive with all the cunning knowledge of his class. "I told uncle I'd found a first who suited me. I must say, Mr. Fox, he gave me a rough time of it."

As though the wind had veered unexpectedly and taken him aback, Fox saw a side of Staunton's character he had only dimly sensed before, when he had found this strange affinity with the nincompoop as they had talked rowing to Minorca. Percy Staunton had risked the very real displeasure of his uncle, the man from whom his patronage flowed. And yet—and yet Fox guessed information had been given, questions had been passed. He caught at the itchy sensation of the grindstones of the Navy rolling ponderously and remorselessly out of his sight or ken. The idea infuriated him. Always—with the notable exception of Captain Sir Cuthbert Rowlands—he had stood alone. He had never possessed Interest. The only time he had thought himself marrying into a family with Interest to bestow —and the memory of poor dear fat Sophie suddenly blotted down on him like a warm shower—he had run head-first into the beginnings of the troubles that had just this morning finally been laid to rest in his court martial.

"It is very good of you, sir," Fox said, formally. He realised he would have to handle Percy Staunton in ways different from those he had at first envisaged. The man was not another Commander Mortlock; equally, and thankfully, he was not another Commander Sanders. The future looked bright.

If he couldn't contrive a rattling good action and a notable prize and be posted, his name wasn't George Abercrombie Fox!

CHAPTER SEVEN

If the lords commissioners of the Admiralty were insane enough to place nincompoops like Percy Staunton in command of expensive and fragile frigates like *Furieuse* they were shrewd enough to see the ship herself was run by crusty old shellbacks who knew their trade backwards.

The Master, Mr. Burlington, met with Fox's approval.

The bosun, Mr. Sneyd, worried Fox, for *Furieuse* was not presented in the way Fox knew she could be. Something was wrong in that department, and he'd find out soon enough, and heads would roll. Any fancy notions of obtaining a warrant for Barnabas, he felt, would come to nothing. Barnabas wanted to stay as he was, an A.B., out of question-fire.

The Gunner and the Carpenter were two solid reliable men. Mr. Jones and Mr. O'Hare had served in ships of the Navy for so long it seemed their fingers and toes had grown into the planking.

The other warrant and petty officers were gone over in their turn by Fox. Something was rotten with this ship, and if the obvious cause might seem to be because her captain was a ninny, Fox knew this was not so. There were many ships with captains far worse than Staunton. Haining, presumably, must take the chief blame. He just did not have the wherewithal to lift a ship, turn her from a collection of wood and iron and canvas and men into a live spirited fighting animal of the sea.

Fox knew he did have that wherewithal and knew how to apply it. The problem was simply one of degree. Hatred for him could be altered into fear and respect. That was all he asked for. He didn't like the men and he didn't care if they didn't love him, he was no Nelson, or so he thought. He just wanted them to do as he told them, to do it right and to do it bloody quick.

From the very first Staunton took him into his confidence. Fox supposed it was hardly in the man's nature not to have done so, for he seemed so open and frank; but Fox never had trusted one of these gilded scions of the aristocrisy, nor even old Lord Kintlesham, and he didn't intend to start now. Orders would be coming down for a cruise, and all that Staunton knew was that he was just as anxious as Fox to lay his hands on prize money.

Prize money.

Yes, well . . . It was an astonishing thing; but Fox realised that his desires now lay beyond mere prize money. He fretted he had lost the loot from that nefarious raid of his and the burning and loss of *Princessa Cristina Maria* was criminal. His own men had hinted that one of Staunton's hands from *Pylas* had caused that desolation.

If they had, it fitted.

But—this matter of mere money. He intended to make, in whatever way he could, money to send back home; that was as much a part of his life as the way of the wind and the scent of the sea; but he felt this stirring of other emotions. He had always felt that being posted would never come his way, no matter that he liked to dwell on that glorious occasion. But; he was the first lieutenant of a frigate commanded by a young man full of the highest expectations. Now, in the normal way that would not have been a good thing, for Staunton would simply be posted on to bigger and better commands, leaving a trail of disappointed first lieutenants behind him. He wasn't going to do that to Fox. No, bigod!

The quicker they got to sea and fought the action that would bring his posting the better.

He didn't believe in it, of course. He had felt something like this when sweet fat Sophie had swooned in his arms for love, and called him her darling Foxey, and her father had talked widely of an Earldom. He had more than half believed he was on the way, then. This time he just wouldn't allow anything to foul it up.

Having occasion to go ashore to distribute a purse of gold where it would do the most good—no one in their right minds called this little habit bribery or corruption—oiling, it might be termed, or the dropsy, or a little easing of the ways. Like any thrifty storehouse keeper the superintendents of the various yard departments never did like parting with the items in their yards to the King's ships who needed those items to fight the war. If it came to push of pike Fox was perfectly prepared to take a party of his desperadoes over the wall of the yard and steal what he needed for his ship.

As the first lieutenant of a smart thirty-six he had taken a ship's boat whereas lesser mortals must needs hire a bumboat from the shore. He went up into the town feeling remarkably well-pleased with himself and with life in general. One drawback to this new existence, so fine, so free, so wonderful, was the loss of Carker and Grey as immediate subordinates. He hadn't really thought about it. But there were a tidy few midshipmen in *Furieuse*, as well as a proper complement of Master's Mates; Carker and Grey were merely two

69

among many. Strange, how that made a material difference to his enjoyment of the day, the sunshine, the passing people of Port Mahon, the pretty girls.

That reminded him of the Turkish girls in the harem they had rescued from the French and who had performed so nobly for him in F.P.B.B. Most had gone with Mustafa Murad, chorbaji of the jemaat, aboard the Turkish frigate. Ten had hidden in the old *Maria.* Fox chuckled. He had heard that the nine Turkish girls they had brought in had been sent to Palermo for onward transmission to Constantinople. Nine. He wondered just which randy devil had taken the other into his protection.

Mind you, if she was aboard *Furieuse* and Fox found her, her protector would have to be flogged.

That made him think of Angelique Labiche. She had found titled friends in Mahon, French Royalists like herself, and had settled down nicely. He pushed thoughts of Angelique away. The task, which in other circumstances would have been infernally difficult on this bright morning of cheer and promise, he accomplished with despatch. Having completed his business any thoughts of Angelique were further dispelled by the dark eyes and pointed glances of the Spanish girl serving wine in the bright sun as Fox halted to partake of a little liquid refreshment.

The British sailor must always be kept away from liquor unless, as at one bell, it was under the most rigorous supervision. But Fox was an officer. So he could drink when he chose. He had tended to drink far less since that time he'd been knocked down in the filthy alley in Plymouth and been left naked in his shirt, to be scooped up by the press gang. Now he quaffed a little light wine, and looked at the girl's ankles and breasts, and leaned back, and felt as near content as he would ever be.

70

Greenery pleasantly shaded the terrazzo. He drank with a delighted appreciation of all the luck that was sure to come his way now. Percy Staunton had invited him to a party at Don Salvator Hernando's villa, a gambling party, and Fox looked forward to another of his pleasures in life. Good food, good wine, not-so-good women, and cards that obeyed his sleight of hand —yes, that was the life.

And then—away on a cruise with a fine fast thirty-six under him. Bigod! But it was good to be alive.

Even if they were sent on convoy duty, a fate he thought hardly likely to befall an admiral's nephew, somehow or other he'd force an action. He felt it. This time, he was aiming at rarefied targets away and beyond mere prize money.

A hat.

Yes, deuced if he wouldn't!

A new hat.

The naval tailors would be glad to sell him a fine new hat.

The wine made everything roseate and glorious as G. A. Fox rolled away to buy himself a brand new hat, with a proper shape, and a gleaming new black cockade, and beautifully lined, and fit for an admiral— with a little additional gold trim.

The transaction passed in something of a blur; he paid out some more of the gold—if it was his own or Staunton's he wasn't by this time quite clear—and clapped the new hat on his head. It felt hard. He bundled his old abortion under his arm and walked out with a fawning clerk opening the door for him.

From the naval outfitters the coffee house held no charms for Fox. He walked back, feeling the weight and sobriety of his new hat. He had dived deeper into debt against the gold he owed his hands, gold they had looted together, gold they did not know existed, for

71

they all must believe everything had gone down with the old *Maria*. That gold was strictly illegal. Too late now to declare it, as he had sworn never to do. It was part and parcel of loot, of finding loose valuables lying about the upper deck, the immemorial right of the fighting sailor.

Wearing this fine new hat the fancy took him to pay a call on Angelique Labiche. He had discovered her name—what she was Countess of, spurning the stripping of her titles by the revolution, and disdaining the title citoyenne. Fox disliked her for that. A merveilleuse and an incroyable—they'd have made a dashing pair strolling down the Champs-Elysees! Although, when that fashion had come in on the trail of terrible violence Fox had hardly been in a position to join in, to ogle the girls walking naked down the Champs or to join in the frenzied dancing in any of Paris's six-hundred-and-forty dance-floors.

Madame la Comtesse d'Arachon—that was who Angelique Labiche was. Rather, that was who she had been. The red, white and blue had more than a trifle severed the jugular vein of the lilies—and a bloody good thing too, according to the testament of G. A. Fox, Esqr., never uttered aloud, drunk or sober.

As to that, his plumb line inclined raffishly to the far-gone side. He rolled most jocosely as he lumbered along in the sunshine. Drink had to be drunk when available. Any horny-handed sand-paper-throated Jack Tar could tell you that. With a curse.

He'd call on Angelique—Angela the Bitch, as he remembered—and maybe she'd give him dinner and a fresh bottle. They might tumble about on a bed spread with white silken sheets, scented with lavender, mellow in the glow of discreet candles. He'd never forget that night in the great deserted cabin of the old *Maria*. She was a funny girl . . .

72

These confounded new breeches of his were damned tight.

He far preferred wearing an old pair of white trousers, loose enough not to impede him comfortable. But, breeches and magnificent new hat, they went together. As to a new uniform frock, well, when he'd made his killing he'd buy half a dozen and have his huge, massive, heavy, gleaming, golden, glorious epaulettes sewn on every damned one of 'em, bigod, he would!

George Abercrombie Fox halted as a set of iron-barred railings impeded his progress.

Damned iron bars! He rattled them impatiently. They penetrated his consciousness enough to make him understand he was not drunk. He was happy. Atmosphere, pleasure, the sunshine, the sound and smell and sights of the land had worked on him, and the wine—a copious amount, to be sure, to be sure—had worked on these delightful surroundings. He was just a little merry, that was all. He was all primed for a romp with Angelique. That was the good news he would bring her.

He fumbled the gates open. A tree-lined driveway, quite short but curving so that the villa of this rich Royalist family lay out of the sight at the end, invited him onward.

He ambled along, breathing deeply, his battered old hat under his arm, his five-ball sword dangling from his left hip from its strap under his coat and over his right shoulder. He smelled the aromas of bushes and shrubs, strange Mediterranean growths of lushness and profusion so much more exotic than the familiar rushes of his boyhood marshes.

A man stepped from the bushes directly ahead.

Fox stared at him, coming to a halt.

A man-o'-war's man. That was plain from his round

blue jacket, his red-striped trousers, the red and white kerchief about his head, the short pigtail. He had a flattened nose. He was big, over-topping Fox by six inches. One glance Fox took—and, as ever, in that glance had weighed the man and knew he could take him, if needs be—and then he strode on again, expecting the man to step aside and deferentially knuckle his forehead.

The man did not move.

Fox halted again, astonished. He heard a scraping of feet on the gravel at his back and half turned. Arms like six-inch hawsers clapped around his waist, trapping his own arms, and a second pair of arms clenched about his neck.

Pure astonishment overcame Fox for a single drunken moment.

He gaped.

The man-o'-war's man stepped forward and hit Fox in the stomach.

A spout of wine gushed from Fox's lips, wine and vomit and bile, splashing the man.

"The filthy son-offa-bitch!"

The man hit him again.

Fox got a knee up and kicked; but the man dodged, his ugly flat-nosed face vicious, clouted Fox across the head.

A voice rapped out, hard, confident, strong; the voice of a naval officer perfectly accustomed to command.

"Don't knock the bastard senseless! I want him to suffer!"

Fox shook his head and listened to Bow Bells dying. He twisted and bent and then straightened with a tremendous opening surge of his arms and shoulders and chest. The arms gripping him slackened and in that instant Fox pivoted and kicked. He knew where to

74

kick. The first man who had gripped him shrieked and doubled up, his face green. Fox lashed out again; but a fourth man darted in, thrusting, and Fox toppled over. His new hat fell off and rolled. He struggled up, striking out, feeling his knuckles and feet connecting with targets both soft and hard.

But there were at least eight of them. They closed in.

Fox was down. He saw a crazily distorted picture of trousered legs surrounding him, of heavy shoes stomping over his new hat to get at him. He rolled. A shoe-cap caught him in the ribs. He whoofed and tried to push up and a fist smashed him back.

He could look up and see the sky, bright—bright!

Captain Lemuel Stone leaned down over him.

"I am not going to have you killed, Fox, you black bastard! My lads are going to rough you up a little!"

Fox blurted words, the vomit vile on his lips.

"You'll be broke for this, Toady!"

"Hit him!"

Fox was duly hit.

"They'll break you and dismiss—" A fist smashed into his mouth.

"Oh, no, Fox, oh no they won't. No one will know. There are no witnesses. I am quietly in *Lynx* at this moment. Whoever beat you up, Fox, you filthy little jumped-up heap of offal, it could never have been me."

Fox let out a sound that might have been a snarl or a curse; hardly a scream.

"I'll teach you who your betters are, Fox! I'll show you! I'll teach you not to forget your place. You'll be sorry you spoke up against me, or Commander Sanders. Oh, yes, Fox, you black bastard, you'll be sorry."

Toady Stone was wrong about that. There was no

would be about it. Fox was only sorry he hadn't pushed Stone over the side when he had the chance.

If the chance came again—as it might!—he wouldn't hesitate this time.

They hauled him upright and held onto his arms and the man with the flat nose kept hitting him in the stomach. This man's eyes held a glazed, fey look that told of deep inner sickness. He licked his lips, which drooped in a rick of pleasure each time he hit Fox. Fox's guts hardly belonged to him any more.

The thought occurred to him, as the bright sunshine dimmed, that if the positions were reversed, and it had been he, G. A. Fox, urging on Barnabas, or Ben, or Josephs or Wilson or any of his own cutthroats to hit Lemuel Stone, they would have done so with the same relish as this man of Stone's hit him. This was true. This was the way of the world.

There lay the true horror.

He sagged now, hovering on the verge of unconsciousness.

They had been clever enough not to knock him out; Stone wanted him to suffer.

By God! He was suffering!

At the end Stone stepped up and thrust a coarse thumb against Fox's eyelid and lifted. Fox could just see him.

"You remember, Fox, you whoreson, you remember."

And Lemuel Stone struck him and then the bright sunshine altogether faded.

CHAPTER EIGHT

Two days later the bruises still wealed purple and angry about Fox's middle; but he was otherwise unaffected as to body for Lemuel Stone's bully-boys had cunningly left his face unmarked. It would have taken considerably more than a mere fist to mark Fox's face seriously, for his beaked figurehead thrust like the wooden carvings of a first rate, but, all the same, the desire to deal privately with jumped-up Lieutenant Fox remained the reason for that. His body would recover; as for his brain, that was hardened already with the injustices of the world to take the incident as just one more mark in his book of remembrance. God help Stone if he caught him in the right circumstances . . .

The duties devolving on a first lieutenant of a frigate could be discharged by Fox—or any other efficient fighting sailor of the Royal Navy with like experience —with a complete knowledge of his profession. *Furieuse* began to alter. An atrocious banging of mess kits and cups and plates broke out on the gundeck forrard, causing Captain Staunton to rush on to his quarterdeck, clutching a pistol, his hair dishevelled, expecting mutiny at the very least.

Fox calmed him down.

"We'll hear all about it in due course, Sir. The Master-at-arms will inform us. The mess cooks have discovered one of their number with light fingers, or in some other way being dishonest, and have convened a cooks' court on him. Take no notice, for, damme, sir, the men are their own best policemen when it comes down to it."

"Very well, Mr. Fox. If you say so, for believe me, I'm deuced taken with your ways, Mr. Fox. Lay me horizontal if you ain't makin' *Furieuse* into the kind of ship I always fancied." He cast a sharp glance at Fox. "Your side, sir? You winced—nothing serious, I hope? Not too many oranges, or grapes—"

"An old wound," said Fox, bravely, taking his hand away from that revolting little swell of his belly. "Nothing to worry about, I do assure you, sir, much though I value your concern."

Staunton took himself off, carrying his pistol as though the thing had suddenly grown from his fingers, all unknown to him. Well, there was something to be said, sometimes, for this long-winded way of talking, filled with subordinate clauses and parentheses and the euphemisms of the time. Fox preferred a harder talk. He used the demotic. It fitted him. But, when he needed to, he could, with all the aplomb and habitual casualness of your true buck talk with the accents of the nobs. Now he returned to the great and consuming joy of the morning.

Letters.

A whole packet, sealed and intact, straight off the cutter from Gibraltar. Marvellous!

Although, to be sure, all the news was not good. Susan wrote that their mother kept well, always insisting on doing more than she should, that the younger girls were behaving themselves, although Charlotte cherished an ambition—a wicked ambition, so Susan said—of becoming an actress. This was a mortal sin, so far as Susan, the upright, the prim, the one who ran the family, saw it.

Archie did not write; but Susan confided that he was still dreaming of shooting King George and over-

78

turning the whole evil system. Fox carefully cut that section of the letter out—infuriatingly it clashed in the cross-written lines with news about Bert and Captain Rupert Colborn. But he dare not risk words like that being found in writing on him or in his effects. Susan should have known better. But, she wrote, the harvest of this year of 1799 was going to be disastrous. If what happened in 1795 and 96 recurred, everyone was in for a lean time.

Fox caught his breath at the implications.

The harvest had failed in 1795. The price of bread had gone mad. A quartern loaf cost over ninepence-halfpenny, and increased again in 1796. In 97 and 98 it had gone to sevenpence three-farthings or so. What it was likely to do now, or in 1800, God alone knew. It might rise over a shilling. The idea of paying a shilling or more for a quartern loaf filled Fox with horror.

More and more land was being enclosed for agriculture; but it was poor stuff and wouldn't have been looked at had not England been at war.

A letter from Godwin that had followed him around the seas from his *Duchess* days contained the sad information that Mary had died. There was a daughter, and Fox was to visit just as soon as he could on stepping ashore in England. Fox felt the nostalgic pungency of olden days. They had argued over the 'Enquiry' and Fox had held out that violence—his kind of violence, the Foxey brand of violence—might serve both their ends admirably; but it had been to no avail. Fox fully understood—or conceived he did—the creed of non-violence; but he was fighting a maniacal Corsican, master of confusion and vendetta, in the service of a king his own brother would have given his right arm to blow up.

Selah!

Fox rubbed his side, and cursed, and went to survey what Parsons had managed to do with his new hat.

"Ohmygawd, sir," said Parsons, as Fox stormed into his screened off cabin off the gunroom.

"Guilty conscience, hey, Parsons? What's the hullabaloo?"

Parsons would have known before the Master-at-arms.

"A mess cook dipping his thumb again, heh?"

"No, sir, begging your pardon, sir."

Parsons looked strange. He held Fox's new hat and a single glance told Fox that the hat was new no more. It was more ruined—if that was possible—than his own old abortion. But it was not the hat that made Parsons look like that.

"Well, out with it!"

"It were young Ben Ferris, sir." Then the story tumbled out.

One of the hands from *Lancebrook*—an able-seaman and therefore one who should have known better—had been shouting his mouth off about the new first lieutenant. He had laid a rough edge to him. Here Parsons swallowed, and cast his eyes aloft, and the worried look on his face trebled in volume, depth and feeling. Mr. Fox, it was said, was the real rightest rottenest bastard in the whole navy.

"So I am, Parsons," said Fox. "Go on."

Parsons swallowed and stuttered out: "So Ben 'it 'im, sir. Right in the breadbasket."

"Did Ben kick him as he went down?"

"No, sir—"

"Idiot."

"Aye aye, sir."

"So—what was the fuss?"

"There'd have bin bloody murder, sir; but Barnabas and Josephs and one or two more stepped in. Then

80

the ship's corporal hove up, and the buzz went the Master-at-Arms was acomin'—so we turned it into a cooks' court."

"Clever sods. We, Parsons? We?"

Parsons had the grace to lower his eyes. "Well, sir, begging your pardon, there was a feller there straight off the slop ship. Bin saying things. I did 'it 'im sir, begging your pardon."

Fox glared at his servant.

My God! What was the navy coming to? First his own officers ripped the topmasts out of a frigate, and now his men brawled in the tween decks. But—officially he could do nothing, and he wanted to do nothing. "Right you are, Parsons. I've forgotten all this. Just see the word gets forrard, will you? Raccoons."

Parsons understood.

But—Fox was dissatisfied.

"There's one thing you can spread. Scuttlebutt. We are no longer Lancebrooks, or Pylases or Raccoons. We're all Furieuses. Tell Ben that. Furieuses. We're all in it, together, up to our necks." His frightful face screwed up into a hideous grimace. "And now, you poxed apology for a ninny—clear out! And leave that thing that looks like a hat!"

"Aye aye, sir!" yelped Parsons and as he fled Fox heard him say under his breath: "Ohmegawd! *Ohmegawd!*"

All Furieuses. Well, the men would soon get their English tongues around that and come up with some approximation to it. Eggs and Bacon for Agamemnon. Yes—and as to the official blind eye; he could have taken notice, of course he could. But that wasn't Fox's way.

He threw the hat onto his cot. The thing was hideous.

He had bought it and worn it in pride and glory; and then he'd been struck down and foully beaten. He

81

was back to his own old hat with its sabre-cut once more.

After Stone had knocked him out his men must have dragged him into the bushes. When he'd revived he'd been able to walk. Stone was quite right. No one would believe Fox if he told his incredible story. Beatings were common enough, handed out by bully-boys employed by the nobility and the rich; but they wouldn't credit a captain of a King's Ship having a simple lieutenant beaten up. Or, if they did credit it, they would do nothing. And 'they' meant all those with golden epaulettes and gold on their uniforms and hats.

Well, all those aristocratic nincompoops knew what they could do.

Although—Percy Staunton, the honourable Percy Staunton, favourite nephew of Admiral Staunton, son of Lord Smithgate—was one of those aristocratic nincompoops. Fox conceded he wouldn't wish our Percy a broken neck. Not at all.

The same Percy Staunton, beaming with pleasure at the coming evening's entertainment, clattered somewhat loosely down into his barge to join Fox in the sternsheets that evening. He had received no permission to sleep out of his ship, so would have to be back before the night was out; George Abercrombie Fox had his mind set on, among other things, the delectable Rosaria, and would fabricate some excuse. Come the morning he'd have a tidy old night behind him when he hauled his carcase aboard a bumboat. Bigod, yes!

Staunton looked a positive glory in his full dress. His epaulettes twinkled. The gold lace around his collar and cuffs and tail coat pockets glowed with that deep refulgence that spoke eloquently of quality. The nap of his coat bristled. His cheerful, flap-eared,

82

pop-eyed, chinless face gleamed with a general well-being and a spaniel-like anticipation of joys to come. Fox sourly wondered what quality of cardplayer he was, what his nerve as a gambler. Probably he was a plunger. A plunger would suit his asinine ideas of honour.

"Damme if it ain't a most jolly evenin', Mr. Fox!"

"Yes, sir, most pleasant."

"I hear tell the signorinas is a deuced handsome stable, Mr. Fox."

"Oh, aye, they ride well."

The barge skipped over the smooth water. The whole crowded anchorage slid past. Over on the green hills of the north shore the wind blew with the scents of the Mediterranean. The barge crew wore impeccable blue jackets, white piped at the seams, and red trousers. Their straw hats shone with the lustre of much administration of elbowpolish. Fox studied them dourly. They were all Pylases—or ex Pylases, rather, remembering his strictures to Parsons. They seemed a handy enough bunch. Lieutenant Greaves, who had been first of the ship, and who had died in the fire in the old *Maria,* must have lavished a disproportionate amount of time on his captain's barge crew. That, surmised Fox, was the way to impress both the captain and his uncle, the admiral.

Fox had left them strictly alone, beyond telling Macey, the cox'n, to keep them up to scratch or, captain's crew or no captain's crew, he'd give them all red-checked shirts at the gangway. He watched stroke, Lestock, sharply, for on stroke depended the rhythm of the crew. Lestock, a big-chested man with a fine head of tallow hair, pulled with a will. Well, Fox would have given a deal to have seen Josephs there—or even poor big stupid old Affleck.

At the steps Staunton rose as was proper to be first

out of the boat. His sword gave him some trouble, investigating the back of the thigh of one leg and the shin of the other. Fox gave him a hefty shove that sent Staunton reeling onto the stone. He managed to stay upright, caught his hat, swathed around with his sword and then, feeling Fox's grip on his arm, quieted.

"All to rights, sir," said Fox. He felt like a nursery nanny wiping sticky bottoms.

That sword was a dainty piece of jewellery. A small sword, with a thin straight blade, not overlong, it had been mounted with gracefully-curved quillons, and cups, and a pommel shaped like a Grecian amphora, from which the tang protruded in a way Fox considered spoiled the whole effect. But then, Fox with his usual intolerance found little favour in almost all methods of dealing with the tang. It was essential—otherwise the first devil you spitted would run off with your blade through his guts and leave you grasping the hilt— but it had to be carefully engineered into the whole design. His own five-ball sword, given him by Lord Kintlesham in the days when he was Sophie's hero and intended, had dealt with the tang neatly. But, even so, graceful and elegant though his five-ball was, it was sadly old-fashioned these days. The new fashions, as shown by that icy supercilious bastard Aiken, were thicker and heavier and rounded and altogether more brutal.

Fox understood that to be the result of the war.

Wordy would have known how to phrase that one. He missed hearing from him, as he missed a letter from Rupert; but the packet had contained no letters from them.

Don Salvator welcomed them with open arms. Both senior officers ashore at the same time from the same ship worried him as little as it worried Fox, for bigod, if anyone fouled up his ship whilst he was gone Fox

84

would cut them into little pieces. Staunton burbled and cooed and the ladies descended and Fox looked around for wine and food.

Anyway, he'd pack our Percy off to *Furieuse* in good time. Let the lad have his drink and his hand of cards and his ogle. Fox doubted he was still a virgin, although it was not unknown in that callow kind of fellow; but Percy was due back aboard tonight and Fox meant him to get there safe and sound. He understood well enough that this was part of the duties expected of a lieutenant charged with the well-being of an admiral's favourite nephew.

Fox stared about him with the slow, comfortable appraisal of a Mongol Khan surveying a Christian city.

Soft candle light, soft female shoulders, soft meats, soft furnishings and sofas and draperies of curtains screening alcoves for the softer pursuits of life; the soft life, here, truly, and so it was, as always, that Fox was vividly reminded of real life, of the shriek of the wind and the frightful force of water shipped green, of canvas shredding, of men spinning helplessly overside, of the plunge and shudder of a ship in great seas.

Well, maybe he was being ungrateful to Don Salvator.

Captain Cloughton came across the crowded room, carrying a wine glass that he emptied on his way. Automatically Fox took a fresh glass from Alfredo's tray as the man passed, sweating in the candles' light, held it out to Black Dick.

"Quick, as ever, Fox, you young devil."

Cloughton drank. His pot-bulge bulged. His eyes bulged. His calves bulged. But he had saved Fox's bacon; Fox was convinced of that. Now Cloughton rolled those protuberant eyes towards Percy Staunton.

"Yes, sir. Shall you care to have him introduced?"

"I think so, Mr. Fox."

When Fox manoeuvred Staunton away from some concoction of sea food and two painted women with fans disputing possession, and trundled him up to Cloughton, he was still trying to fathom what lay in Black Dick Cloughton's mind.

The conventional civilities were made, Cloughton and Staunton spoke together, ignoring Fox; Fox made himself scarce.

He took his time eating only those delicacies he fancied. Being stationed in the Mediterranean usually conferred one enormous advantage on a ship's company, for fresh food could be more easily obtained than it could by, for example, any of the poor devils on blockade duty outside Brest. He rubbed the two fingers of his left hand across his stomach. Hard tack and salt pork would trim that, for him, unlike so many of his contemporaries who grew fat on ships' rations. He drank sparingly. Later, after the cards, he would indulge. As it was, he intended to play perfectly straight. Ahead of him lay a future glorious with opportunities, and a little quick cash now meant little—and he found the enormity and the impossibility of that thought mocking him. He, G. A. Fox deliberately turning down the chance to make money! Truly, his sights were set far higher than ever before.

The captain who had left *Furieuse* to Staunton must have gone onto better things; for a frigate command was heaven. Fox could feel that mantle of good-humour settling over him as, glass in hand, and with an affable nod towards Don Salvator, hard at work conducting his business with Captain Falconer, he made his way towards the card room.

A stab of memory of that card game in Lord Kintlesham's house in Palermo recurred. That had

86

been when he'd collected two duels in an evening, after carrying out a hectic sea-rescue. That fortune-hunting bastard Lord Fotherby had chickened-out of his duel, and, the callous balgskite, had taken Sophie off with him to England. The other duel had taken place after the Marchese di Perogna, Benedetto Fogazzaro, had accused Fox of cheating. Fox had not been cheating. However odd that might have been, Fox had been playing fairly, and a challenge and a duel had resulted. He shook the feeling off and straightened his neckcloth, the movement pressing the cloth of his old coat to his arm and reminding him he did not carry his little hide-away gun in his sleeve.

Maybe he would not be called upon to deal with a rat this evening.

A considerably larger number of guests than Fox had expected had been asked and the rooms of Hernando's villa rang with laughter and loud conversation, with the strains of a small string ensemble Don Salvator had engaged, fiddling away in their balconied alcove. Candles burned everywhere. Fans fluttered and faces grew brighter and more flushed. Fox wended his way very carefully to the card room, not wishing to be distracted by white shoulders and arms, by roguish eyes, this early. First he must assuage this desire to test his skill against the locals, then he must pack Staunton off in his barge—then he could pick up by conquest whatever the fates decreed him.

The first person he saw when he entered the card room was Captain Lemuel Stone.

Stone sat slumped on the edge of his little gilt chair. His face showed the unmistakable signs of a gambler in the throes of his passion, hurling his cards down as though each was a tablet brought down by Moses, his face scarlet, his eyes feverish, sweat slicking his upper lip and trickling down his cheeks. His legs were

87

twisted back under the chair and his sword thrust beyond, inconveniently to the passerby. Fox approved of that. He did not like people ogling his cards over his shoulder, either.

Then—of the players around the green table his eyes snapped up the cameo of the woman sitting at Stone's left hand. She laughed a great deal, with much fan fluttering, her white-gloved hands dealing nonetheless with delicate and professional skill with her cards. Fox saw those dancing black ringlets, those wide violet eyes, all the beauty and vivacity of her and he remembered the hauteur, the pride, the knowledge of blood-breeding that formed an inescapable part of her birthright. And, too, he remembered Angelique Labiche with her lips moist and parted, trembling, lying voluptuously on the priceless carpet from Kairouan in the great aft cabin of the old *Maria*. My God! She had been passionate! He rubbed two reflective fingers across his stomach and a flickering ring of purple and black hovered around his left eye.

Stone and Angelique. Well, for all her French Royalist friends, she would need find all the protection she could. He had been on the way to see her when Stone and his bully boys caught him. Maybe, through the pasteboards and their baffling pips, he might get a little back at Stone. Yes, bigod! He'd fleece Stone tonight. He'd take the swine for all he had.

Angelique glanced up from the green table and saw him, and her face lost all its colour, and her eyes devoured him; then the fan fluttered up and concealed all her lower face so that only those violet luminous eyes glowed upon him.

He'd show her Toady Stone in a new light tonight! He'd fleece the bastard!

A voice spoke at his elbow, an elegant smooth-faced man was rising, his hand extending.

"Captain Fox! This is a surprise, sir, a most un-expected meeting."

Fox stared into the dark smiling face of Benedetto Fogazzaro the Marquese di Perogna, the man who had accused him of cheating.

CHAPTER NINE

Fox shook the proffered hand firmly. "Marquese."

Fogazzaro stared at him in a most deucedly odd way. This was the man Fox had shot in the right arm. Then, at the close of the duel, Fox had said: "I did not cheat. I won fair and square. I think you should know that."

"My handshake, Captain Fox, was firm enough, yes?"

Fox nodded.

"I am gratified that no permanent harm resulted, marquese."

Somewhere in the other room a man's loud and port-winey-voiced complaint echoed in. "Damned devilish idea of Billy Pitt's. Taxing our income—taking the hard-earned money out of the mouths of our wives and children—By God, sir, this war will starve us all before we're through."

Fox's mercurial mind fleeted with contemptuous thoughts; fat chance of that bloated speaker starving, paying income tax at all. Billy Pitt had trotted out his income tax scheme in December last year, and now it was beginning to bite. Good luck to him, said Fox, despite what he'd done to the Navy with his damned Quota Men. Income tax might bite into his own miserable pay a little; practically no officer could live on his pay, and all the litttle dodges of allowances and other payments plied a brisk trade through every strata of the Navy.

"You have not forgotten me, then, Captain Fox?"

"No, marchese. It is Lieutenant Fox, if you please."

Benedetto Fogazzaro must have been conscious that the other card players were looking at him, that Madame la Comtesse had paled and reacted to Fox's entrance—her face now blushed with a vivid painfulness—and that Captain Stone was sneering in a strange indrawn way whilst he flicked a card between his fingers; but the marchese was a marchese and used to doing what he wanted to do and damn anyone else.

Fox guessed, also, that his own defiance of this man had intrigued the Italian nobleman. Fox let his breath out, glanced around, bowed to Angelique, completely ignored Stone, and said: "Mr. Fox it is now, marchese. My command burned—after she was taken over by someone else," and sat down in the seat facing Stone.

Angelique's fan fluttered violently. Could it be merely the entrance of a tarpaulin lieutenant that had agitated her to this degree?

Fogazzaro resumed his seat. "My deepest regrets on the loss of your command, Capt—ah—Mr. Fox."

Fox's Italian had improved considerably since he had last seen Fogazzaro; but he continued the conversation in English. He felt a certain intrigue about this Italian; he would have expected him to be icily polite and planning revenge. Instead, he was going out of his way to show friendship. Fox nodded to the cards. "I heartily wish you better success than the last time we played."

"Costa trove! I share your desires, Mr. Fox, a thousand-fold."

"Are we here to play cards or not?" demanded Stone. He brayed the words, and then bent his head immediately as Angelique whispered in his ear, hidden by her fan. Fox would dearly liked to have taken her out and —Then he recollected himself. She was beautiful, a

91

countess, once more ensconced among her Royalist friends. Her dress, a marvel of a pale ivory material, set her dark beauty off perfectly; it had cost a lot more than his pay he had been worrying about just now.

She was no longer the tempestuous beauty who had come to the great aft cabin of the three-decker.

Cards were played. Fox let the game laze along, studying. Other players joined in; but Fogazzaro did not leave. Fox's winnings, because he played with skill, mounted; but then, so did the heap of gold on the green table before Stone. Fox remembered Toady Stone. He intended to rook the bastard; but if he cheated with less than an exquisite skill then Benedetto Fogazzaro might believe that Fox was the cheat he had once dubbed him, might then go raving mad.

The abrupt realisation came to Fox that the setting for this operation was all wrong. Soft candle light, the sheen of beautiful women's bare shoulders, fans and feathers, good wine in priceless cut-glasses—no, he did not want the great imposing and artificial gambling scene here. Perhaps down in the after cockpit with the vomit and excreta staining the planking, a purser's dip stinking, men and boys shrieking and fighting all over them, the groan and working of a ship at sea and the rush of the water alongside. Yes, perhaps there he might have enjoyed taking Toady Stone to the cleaners.

If Fogazzaro spotted him performing a trickly sleight of hand—Goddammit to hell! Was he or was he not George Abercrombie Fox? Did he or did he not owe Toady Stone? Had he or had he not faced Fogazzaro in a duel and shot the man? In short—was Fox no longer Fox?

In immediate answer he riffled the deck, cut and dealt with a pure flowing beauty of motion that sent the cards like flying fish into their places, settling down with tiny inaudible sighs. Stone lost a tidy proportion of his gold on that hand, and swore, and said that, damme, he didn't believe it.

Remorselessly, Fox went on. He left Angelique and Fogazzaro alone. He had no quarrel with them of the calibre he had with Stone. He took the man. He fleeced him. He rooked him.

Shatteringly, numbingly, infuriatingly—he did not enjoy the doing of it.

Stone pushed back. He looked dreadful.

"I just don't understand it, confound it!" He glared at Fox, across from him. You seem to have done well, Mr. Fox, for yourself. A coincidence?"

Fox went carefully on stacking the gold in neat piles.

"If you have something to say to me—sir—say it." Then, because Angelique was staring at him with those gorgeous violet eyes beseeching him, and her breasts rising and falling within her gown, he added in the form: "I shall be most interested to hear any observations you may care to make—sir."

Stone kept his hands at full-spread on the table edge, his arms at full-stretch pushing him back in the little gilt chair. "I remarked on your damned luck, Mr. Fox." Stone wet his lips. He struggled with himself, Fox saw, wanting to say what he did and yet— unable. Was the bastard still shy, then?

Fogazzaro interrupted, with a laugh, calling for wine, hurling down his cards. "I can tell you, ladies and gentlemen, Mr. Fox is the luckiest man at cards I have ever met. I was once foolish enough to accuse him of cheating. I can assure you, Mr. Fox has no need of cheating."

And the story came out, and the buzz of conversation, and Fogazzaro, with his strict Italian code of honour taking a considerable pride in it all. Fox found a jolt of pleasure take him at the marquese's attitude. If some swash-buckling sod had shot him, he'd be dreaming up ways of shooting back.

'A brave face' the Italians called some aspects of their honour code. Fogazzaro must know what he was doing. But, among an English crowd, his attitude sparked just the right response, and he was, they all agreed, a regular good sport.

Later, Fox took his winnings off, collected Percy Staunton and loaded him into the barge. Macey, the captain's cox'n, clucked his tongue as Staunton almost fell in. He was not drunk, just mellow. Fox stared at Macey. What he was about to do was against almost all the principles of his rascally life. But he had an intuition in these things. He took out the heavy purse of gold.

"Cox'n. You take charge of this for me. Take it straight to the Master. I know exactly how much is there. If any is missing I'll see to it you get a hundred lashes for every piece missing. Got it?"

"Aye aye, sir. I'll take care of it, sir, my oath on it."

"Make it so."

Mr. Midshipman Gruber sat in the sternsheets looking most offended. He was a mere baby, barely thirteen, with a face like an unfired clay jug. "Mr. Gruber! Kindly take that expression off your face! I'll trouble you to wipe that disgusting snot from your nose—not with your sleeve, you—you—" Fox breathed out, hard. "Get the captain aboard safely, Mr. Gruber, or it'll be more than a mastheading, believe you me."

"Aye aye, sir!" squeaked Gruber, appalled.

Fox stood and watched until the barge pulled away. He sighed. Gruber might be a snotty-nosed little tyke; but his family wanted him to go to sea and be an admiral, and he might have his guts blown through his backbone when they were in action. It took all sorts to make a world.

He went back to the party.

Captain Stone was just leaving.

The two men met in the shadowed portico. They were alone.

Fox felt that awful grimace draw down over his face, his lips rick back, that mad glare blaze into his eyes, his jaw go forward. Stone flinched back, his hand going to his sword hilt. His voice slurred, wine-thick.

"You black bastard, Fox! I'll get you—and this time I won't stop—"

Fox recollected himself. He let his right fist drop.

"I may kill you, Toady, yet," he said, and pushed past and so entered Don Salvator's villa. Cloughton came out at that moment and so Fox knew that his hunch had once again saved him. How Stone would have raised the hue and cry if Fox had hit him—as he had fully intended to do—and he was lying retching on the ground, with Fox standing over him, and a senior captain like Cloughton had arrived on the scene.

"G'night, Fox. Don't forget." Black Dick swirled his boat cloak about him grandly. "Let me know, there's a good feller."

Lights flared up, horses' hooves trampled, men called out, Don Salvator was there, bowing and bobbing, happy with the business he had done this night. The party was over. Fox cursed. Angelique Labiche appeared, drawing a huge dark cloak, fur-edged, about herself. Her face floated like a lily above a nighted pool.

"You may share my carriage, Mr. Fox, an' you wish."

Any other man might have said something like: "*Enchanté*, Madame la Comtesse."

95

Fox, about to be Fox, and swing off into the night, paused.

He saw Don Salvator talking to other of his departing guests. He saw Angelique's face gleaming there in the night. He could feel the free full flow of her body beneath her cloak like the feel of blood in his own body. Bigod, yes!

"I shall be very happy, Angelique. I think we have things to talk about."

"Assuredly, *mon brave,* assuredly."

They entered the carriage and before he was fully settled, before the driver had time to flick his whip and cluck, Angelique's lips were against his own, her hands plundering, her body warm and trembling against him.

"Oh, Foxey, Foxey," she moaned. She *was* moaning, her lips against his, her breath hot and sweet on his face, her hands probing and devilish. "Oh Foxey! How I need you."

He kissed her back, and calmed her, and held her close as the horse lurched forward, the carriage jolted, and they rolled away.

Then he said: "And Toady Stone?"

"Is that what you call that horrible man?" They spoke quick idiomatic French, which Fox, deviously, kept tailored to heights unknown to the depths he had frequented in Paris. "What can I do? My money is gone. I am alone, defenceless—"

"But your Royalist friends?"

"Most are like me. There is the count of Carsonois. He is rich and he wants to marry me; but he is withered and ugly and *old*."

"That should be no impediment to a girl like you, Angelique."

"What do you say, hein?"

96

"Nothing. You must live your life. So you gave Toady his marching orders?"

She shivered and clutched tighter. "He revolts me; but I have to live. But, tonight, I was a little mad."

Why should he worry about this one? She was an aristocrat who refused to recognise that French aristocrats were no longer wanted. Her stupid Royalist friends . . . "Marry Carsonois and bolt your door." He chuckled, and grabbed her. "Or marry him and never lock your door and have him in his box inside six months."

"Oh, Foxey . . ."

They rolled up the drive where he had been beaten up and the recollection barely stirred his attention. They made themselves respectable so as to tumble out of the carriage, flit indoors, seize a candle from a puff-eyed maid, run upstairs and tumble onto the bed. The tumble—aye, the tumble—that followed was sweet, as Fox had known it would be.

Let the devil take ships and the sea, just for these few hours of sweetness.

By morning, with the sun splintering in past the closed edges of the blinds, Fox rolled out, groaned, stretched, slapped Angelique on her naked rump, stood up and began to dress.

Angela the Bitch. Well, he felt sorry for her; that was his trouble.

She embraced him before he left. This house, the servants, the carriage, all had to be paid for. Toady Stone would no longer come up to scratch.

"If you are Madame la Comtesse Carsonois, Angelique, let me know. I wish you well."

Her white hand trailed from his own horny brown palm.

"Goodbye, Foxey." She spoke English, caught her-

97

self, swept her hair back, to say, with a catch in her voice: "No, Foxey, *au revoir!*"

"*Au revoir*, Angelique."

As he went down to the steps he thought to himself that, yes, *au revoir* was best. He'd welcome another night like that, bigod. They were few and far between as it was.

Grey with the cutter waited at the steps. His face lit up when he saw Fox. "Orders, sir. We have to weigh and proceed to sea at once. I've been waiting since first light."

Fox stared at him. Cheeky young devil.

CHAPTER TEN

The run to Gibraltar gave Fox some chance to begin the operation of making a crew out of the odds and ends, the rag tag and bobtail, collected into *Furieuse*.

He had been through the essential paperwork with Staunton. A watchbill had been drawn up. All the lieutenants were fit to stand a watch. There were plenty of able seamen, men able to hand, reef and steer. The proportion was uncannily high. Fox had the weird sensation that being an admiral's nephew opened the pot of gold and the cornucopia of hands. He gave the boatswain, Mr. Sneyd, enough rope to hang himself. The other departments functioned very well. Hogan, the old carpenter from those riotous days of *Raccoon*, had not been signed on; but Mr. O'Hare was a fine hard-grained chippy and would uphold the traditions of the service. Mr. Jones the gunner, so Fox received from Parsons, met with Joachim's approval. Fox had long since passed being amazed at his reliance on his own old hands. He had to clamp down on any slightest suspicion that he favoured them over the others.

The question of name was settled satisfactorily.

One morning, with *Furieuse* on the larboard tack, well braced up, the sun shining, the spray sleeting finely, the whole vessel thrumming and humming and cleaving through the sea, Fox strode onto the quarterdeck, cocking his intolerant eye aloft and all around, instantly aware of his situation, how it went with the ship, and what was amiss.

Master's Mate John Carker stood by the binnacle, running sand-glasses against each other, assisted by Midshipman Gruber, nose running as usual. The officer of the watch, Mr. Morgan, third of the ship, effectively prevented Fox from talking in any normal way with Carker. He had to admit it. He missed the ease of comradeship with Carker and Grey. It was not right, it was foolish, it was weakness; but Fox would dearly have loved to be back to those days of *Raccoon* with Grey and Carker and the intricate relationships they were working out. Mind you—he'd want *Furieuse* under him, into the bargain!

A trim to the canvas was required. Mr. Morgan gave the requisite orders in a way that partially satisfied Fox. A bosun's mate was cracking his starter down, and the hands were heaving, and a block caught and confusion suddenly milled.

Fox stepped to the quarterdeck rail.

"Come on, Furieuses!" he bellowed. "Let's see you act like seamen! Cheerily, now!"

The snagged block freed. John Carker, anxious, leaned out, all those months of acute attention as second in command to Fox boiling and seething in him.

"Cheerily, now!" he yelled in the old familiar way. "Come on your Furry-arses, with a will there!"

This really would not do. The good Carker must be bereft of his senses; but Fox had no hesitation in step- ping forward to Carker's side, as though personally inspecting the damage, and roaring it out, so that the officer of the watch, Lieutenant Morgan, would think twice before letting his wrath fall upon a presumptuous master's mate.

"Let's be having you, your Furry-arses!" he sang out.

Ben Ferris, it was, who took it up first. As an old

100

Raccoon he thought he understood the wild ways of Lieutenant Fox. Soon the name had percolated to every part of the ship. That afternoon when the drums thundered and the hands roared up from below with the starters of the bosun's mates whipping around their posteriors, the urgency of the rush was intensified and dramatised by the ferocious bellowing of: "Git along there, you Furry-arses!"

Well, if Eggs and Bacon equalled *Agamemnon,* then Furry-arses did right nobly equal out against Furieuses.

When the noise and confusion subsided, and the inferior officers had reported the men fallen in, and the necessary chain of command carried the word to the first lieutenant, with every man at his quarters, the marines solid aft on the quarterdeck, the gun crews with their equipment by their guns, the waisters where they belonged, in the waist—and shockingly few of them there were, too—Fox could turn with the dignity of twenty four years at sea, cross the quarterdeck and touch his hat to the captain.

"Hands at quarters, if you please, sir."

"Very well, Mr. Fox," said Captain Staunton. He took a few steps up and down, and gazed about, and looked aloft, and caught his lips between his teeth whilst over the whole surging fabric of the ship every man stood silently.

Fox debated carefully. Normally he dived in unhesitatingly. The routine afternoon's evolution of beating to quarters was a vital part of ship discipline, instructing every man, as it did, where he was to run to as though the devil was on his heels with a red hot pitchfork. Fox might not brandish a red hot pitchfork; but he was the devil for these men, and he wielded the awful power of having the captain order a flogging.

101

Carefully, Fox said: "I'd like to exercise the great guns, sir—"

"Excellent, Mr. Fox! A capital notion. Poor Mr. Greaves was for ever having the guns run in and out, quite made my head ache. But I'm sure it's all for the best."

Fox had formed his own opinion of Lieutenant Greaves. He had seen him but the once, when he had come leaping in onto the quarterdeck of the old *Maria,* when Fox had been struck down. Fox had been impressed by the way the man—a man so very much like himself—had said: "Lie easily, Mr. Fox. I'll take over command now." Yes. Mr. Greaves had had our Percy well-trained, had him under his thumb. Greaves wouldn't be asking tacitly for permission to exercise the guns. Well. Fox had formed a strange and unsettling feeling—he dared not call it an affection—for our Percy, and this despite his bitter hatred of all noble authority. Fox dared not admit it. Fox dared not . . ? The whole idea was foolish. Fox would spit in Jervis's eye if his family was at stake.

In a passion he swung about and most intemperately began flinging abuse at the gun crews, the quarter gunners, the midshipmen and Haining and Morgan. The lashings were cast off and the prescribed drill went forward as the guns were run up, a pretence that they fired took place, and were then dragged back to be pretend-loaded and run out once again.

Midshipman Grey stood by his position at the signals locker. As signals midshipman he was comfortably close to Fox. The feeling Fox had for Grey, that limb of Satan, was nothing like the new awareness of affection he felt for Staunton. Fox knew well enough that when Grey was posted—as he would be, probably before Fox, if Fox ever was—there'd be none of this

102

play-acting of meek humility in ranks. Grey would make a damned fine captain.

They were running down to Gib to pick up orders. *Lynx* had left Port Mahon before them—clearly Stone had been going on board when that encounter in the portico had taken place—and Fox just hoped *Lynx* would not be swinging to her buoy in Gib when *Furieuse* railed in.

Conscious of these weakening thoughts. Fox hurled a fresh and volatile set of orders at the signals department, and with a scurry of activity Dillon spurred them on, giving Grey the edge of his tongue. Fox could guess what Grey was thinking in that damned way of his, laughing up his sleeve at this shabby, quaint, shellback old lieutenant Fox of his.

So the run was made, with Fox hammering at the hands to turn them into a semblance of a crew he could take into action.

Furieuse was, as a thirty six, a fine large vessel. She measured nine twenty tons burthen, and was a hundred and forty six feet on the lower deck. Her beam of thirty nine feet nine inches gave ample working space, although Fox had the niggling idea she might have been a little fuller, although he had leaped with his sailorman's eye at her rake when he'd first clapped eyes on her. Being a French prize she was undeniably a fine ship; but the carpenter, Mr. O'Hare, went about with a long face all the time, lugubriously announcing to his crew that the damned Froggies couldn't build a hen-coop, let alone a frigate. This was often the trouble with French ships; beautiful specimens of the naval architect's genius; but cobbled together with green timber and too light scantlings.

As Fox said to Percy Staunton: "We'll drive old Furry-arse, and she'll serve us well. But not for long. One fine day she'll fall apart around our ears."

Whereat Staunton squealed and observed he devoutly hoped he'd be out of the ship that day, lay him horizontal else.

The regulation armament for a thirty six consisted of twenty six eighteen-pounders on the upper deck, eight nine-pounders on the quarterdeck and a couple of twelve-pounders on the forecastle. But, as usual, she was armed above her legend, and the nine-pounders just did not exist. When taken from the French she'd had brave shiny brass thirty six-pounder carronades. The British had given her their own superior iron thirty two-pounder—twelve of them. And two more on the forecastle, to add a little punch forrard.

A fine ship, a good sea-boat, fast and weatherly, was *Furieuse,* with a good thumping punch; but she tended to be wet below, and needing constant attention, and a lottery bet on the exact date of her impending collapse.

An accident occurred on the first occasion Fox decided he might expend a few barrels of the white-grain reconstituted powder he generally detested. He'd spent a tidy amount of Staunton's money in oiling the ways for a supply over what was strictly due to the ship of the red large grain powder that would be used for real work. Never one to neglect stocking up on the tools of his trade, was Foxey.

The evolutions of casting loose the guns, of opening the portlids, of holding the guns level and steady against the heel of the ship, of removing the tompions, of running out the guns, all went smoothly. The gun captains primed. Fox stood watching the ordered activity, his hands tucked up behind his back. At his side Captain Staunton stood in the same attitude, his head perhaps a trifle more thrust forward. Fox watched with the same careful intolerant attention to detail he had cultivated all his life aboard ship. He had once

104

been a powder monkey and had run with his leather bucket of cartridge. He remembered the old *Henrietta*. He could never forget. Nor, for that matter, would he forget *Nicodemus*. And that reminded him of Toady Stone, and he scowled so monstrously that a clear minute was lopped off the men's sweating efforts.

"Fire!"

The flintlocks clashed, sparks flew, the deep thunderous booming smashed across the sea, the smoke jetted and spread and blossomed, and the smell of gunsmoke filled every nook and cranny of him, as though his nostrils opened his whole physical being to a new dimension.

Then the accident happened.

The tackle of number six gun's breechings caught in the block. Instead of rushing with that maniacal hurtling straight backwards, the eighteen pounder hung up aft, slewed, roared, tipped over. It happened in a twinkling. The concussion of the guns hung on the air, drowning the gut-wrenching shrieks of Ordinary Seaman Pontoppidan, a Dane from Odense. The truck of the eighteen-pounder's carriage had run clean over his foot. Pontoppidan, known to his messmates as Ponty, was a popular man. Fox cherished a respect for the Danes, knowing them to be tough, resolute, dogged people with whom he could deal, and Ponty, rated for the moment Ordinary Seaman, was marked out to be rated A.B. within the very near future. Now the poor devil's foot was crushed, because a block and tackle had jammed.

Furieuse carried no surgeon.

The Purser? The boatswain? The carpenter—given that it would be sawyer's job? Fox cursed horribly.

"Mr. Haining! Take over exercising the great guns if you please." Fox caught sight of Sneyd, the bosun, getting set to sling the now manfully silent Dane over

105

his shoulder. "Mr. Sneyd! Have a care! Handsomely with Ponty!"

Other men rushed. Fox cursed them foully back to their stations. He followed the bosun and a bosun's mate as they carried Pontoppidan to the sick-bay, up forward and to starboard.

The men were being driven back to their guns by the master's mates, midshipmen and quarter gunners as he strode forward. Smoke still hung bitterly on the air. He heard someone as he passed say: "That black bastard Foxey knew Ponty's name!"

And the reply: "Old Foxey's got everyone of us sewed up tight, like we wuz in our ammicks with a roundshot."

No time to try to ferret out who had spoken. He wouldn't even bother to ask Midshipman Callaghan who commanded the guns here who had spoken. Fox had already realised that the way these men regarded him reflected the regard of other men he had led into battle. He didn't care if they called him Old Foxey, or that black bastard Fox, just so long as they gave him everything in them, right up to the moment of death and beyond.

"A bad business, this, sir," said Mr. Gyver, the Purser.

"Aye. Get the tar-tub ready. Good pitch, mind! My compliments to Mr. O'Hare," he shouted at a loblolly boy—a certain near-cretin called Absalom—"And I want his finest, keenest saw. Jump!"

Absalom squeaked: "Yes—er, aye aye, sir!" and vanished.

Fox looked down on Ponty, lying on the blanket-spread table. Sunshine shafted in through the opened port forward.

"You'll be all right, Ponty." He took the bottle of rum the Purser offered. "Drink this. All of it."

106

"Aye aye, sir," said Ponty. His English could cope with that response, he was a good man; now he was finished.

"You're not finished, Ponty. Maybe you'll get a warrant as a cook. Nice berth that, Ponty, for a smart lad like you."

The rum glugged out of the bottle. Fox bent and looked at the foot. Well, the lump of raw red gristle and bone and mangled flesh was never a foot. He stripped the red-striped white trouser back. In the loblolly boy's bowl he washed his hands carefully. Mr. O'Hare came in with his saw. Fox took it, breathed in—the smells compounded into an overwhelming aroma of shipboard life and death—and started in.

They held Ponty down; but the rum and his own innate toughness made that portion of the task easy. Fox slivered and sliced away and then sawed through the bone. Speed. The way to amputate was as fast as you could go. He had the foot off in no time at all. Then he swung back to Ponty, looked down at the wide eyes, the sweat-thick forehead, the clamped mouth with still a little rum running down. He cocked his fist and slammed it against Ponty's jaw.

"Into the pitch with it."

After that it would be up to nature. If gangrene set in, no one could do anything, and prayer would be all that was left.

He took a last look at Ponty, breathing deeply, his face ashen, lying in the sick-bay cot; then he ducked his head and went out. Damned stupid block and tackle! He'd have all those responsible answer for this. This wasn't good enough for Fox, bigod, it wasn't!

He'd pulled the skin back as far as he could before cutting, so as to get a good flap to sew up. He hoped to God he'd be in Gib before that had to be subjected to his own scrutiny. Staunton really ought to badger

107

his uncle to get a surgeon for the ship. That caught Fox shrewdly. He was actually calculating out something he wanted and taking into account the high connections of his captain. It might not be novel; but Fox felt the betrayal of all his own iconoclastic resolutions. Doctors were hard to come by in the Fleet—good doctors, that was. The half-baked medical men who did sail were most of them blind drunk all the time.

He was an intolerant man, he knew it, he didn't care; but what he did care about was the well-being of his crew, simply because on them depended his own career and chances of getting his step and of raking in loot for his family.

Any fool of a blind-drunk half-doctor could take off a foot. It was hardly the thing for the first lieutenant. But in the way scuttlebutt travels aboard ship Fox became aware that his action had curiously given him a kind of cachet with the hands. Ironically, the thing that had struck them was that he had known the name of the Dane. Each man now felt that Fox knew his name, individually. The truth was that Fox knew most of them and by the time they reached Gib he would have every man's name, rating and capabilities all neatly filed away in that complex storage-cupboard of a brain of his.

Just before that looked-for event and with the Rock about to burst into view over the horizon, Mr. O'Hare came to Fox with a long face. It was just after two bells in the first dog watch.

"Well, Mr. O'Hare?"

"It's these pesky Froggies, sir. All fine cloathes and skimped stitching." Lord save me from another poetic Hogam! said Fox to himself. The carpenter went on, shaking his head, from which he had removed the Monmouth cap the better to scratch his perplexity. "It's down on the forrard orlop, sir, station H." O'Hare took a breath, about to launch, for the benefit of high-and-mighty deck-lieutenants who knew nothing about naval ship-building, into a long-winded explanation of the midship section as being the dividing line between the fore body and the afterbody of the ship, and that aft of this dead flat the frames were numbered and forward they were lettered.

Knowing all this perfectly well—talk of scarphs and breast hooks and riders, crosspales and first fut-tocks and all the rest of the arcane lore of shipbuilding had dinned into Fox's ears from the moment he was born—Fox said: "I'll come, Mr. O'Hare," and forthwith started off forrard. O'Hare scratched his thatch again, shifted his quid, and followed.

Down in the orlop Fox's nose noticed and ignored the familiar bilge-smells from below; the years had given him a tolerance level and as soon as his nose told him that level had been exceeded he would know something was amiss. The trouble here was of a different kind. The ship groaned with all the familiar and usually unheard wood-noises, which the rush of water past the hull conjoined into a single blended mael-strom. An experienced ear could pick out individual noises, and assign precise reasons and locations to them.

O'Hare brought the lantern carried by one of his carpenter's crew. They all bent over bobbing in the wavering light. Fox looked at station H. Here the French had followed their common fashion of com-bining the rider and hanging knee into one timber. The wood looked to be in poor condition. The lodging knee —that is, the knee that lay in the horizontal plane attaching the deck beam to the frame—had clearly not long to last. The shiverings and the splittings made Fox curse.

"Like below, sir, most o' the bilges is rotten. The

109

Frogs don't seem to have much Compass timber for their futtocks.

Before O'Hare could explain that Compass timber was wood grown when the tree was alive into the special shape needed, Fox growled: "There's only one thing for it, Mr. O'Hare. We'll have to strap it. I take it there are more like this?"

"Oh, aye, sir; but they'll last come Giberalter, sir."

"I see."

The lamp's glare lit the scene, of lowering timber, massive and bulky with power, curved so subtly to give the exquisite lines of *Furieuse*. But of what use all that beauty and sheer and that fine run aft if the wood was not equal to the task?

Again Fox showed his knowledge of the hands.

"Get Rawlinson to forge up a strap, Mr. O'Hare." Rawlinson was the smith. "I'll trust you to keep your eye on any more rubbish like this, Mr. O'Hare. I'll arrange with Cook." He glared around, feeling the surge and heel of the vessel, seeing the serried ranks of riders and hanging knees and all the multiplicity of wood that made up the living fabric of a ship. Whilst he was here he might as well step below the orlop and check the limbers. This long passage, one each side of the keelson, should be left clear and uncluttered so as to allow water free run to the pump well. He went down into the shadowy cavern of the hold, perfectly at home in this place that, he knew, would be most eerie and frightening to a landsman, and told Garrity, one of O'Hare's crew, to lift a limber board. Garrity did so, not without considerable under-the-breath cursing.

Fox peered in the erratic lantern-light.

Water ran freely—and yet—a bundle, something, lay snagged.

"Hook that out, Garrity."

110

Garrity did as he was bid. Poised on the very centre line of the ship, right over the keelson, Fox took the evil-smelling bundle and unwrapped it, spattering foul-water as he did so. A fresh smell cut through the gathered odours.

"I thought so," said Lieutenant Fox, without humour. He turned and smashed the bottle of brandy against the wood. The potent liquid poured out and Garrity licked his lips, and said nothing.

"If they can't find a better hiding place than that," said Fox, and this time he spoke with humour, "they're not good man-o'-war's men at all, at all."

Garrity bobbed his lantern, but said nothing. He was a big wild bog-Irishman, tough as old iron, who could drive an adze deeper than anyone else in the ship.

"Up!"

They climbed back to the orlop and here a breath-less, dishevelled, snotty-nosed Mr. Midshipman Gruber found Fox.

"Please, sir," he piped, and swallowed, and wiped his face.

"Yes, Mr. Gruber?" shouted Fox, looking down on the boy with the hulking seamen pressing in close in the timbered space.

"Please, sir. Mr. Burlington's compliments, sir, and please to tell you Gibraltar's in sight, six points off the starboard beam."

"Thank you, Mr. Gruber." A devil of mischief Fox had forgotten he possessed drove him to add: "Just remember to say your prayers we reach Gibraltar before the bottom drops out."

"Aye aye, sir," squeaked Mr. Midshipman Gruber, and fled.

CHAPTER ELEVEN

Furieuse howled along on the larboard tack, heeling hard over, trying to keep her head within six points of the wind with the spray and spume gusting over her white, and shining dollops of green water curving solidly inboard. She carried topgallants and royals and George Abercrombie Fox stood with his legs wide-braced on her quarterdeck and drove her into the wind and the weather.

The wind screamed in from the west, level and unhampered all the way from America, howling and shrieking through the myriad lines, taut as fiddle strings, clothing *Furieuse's* masts and yards. The braces had been hauled hard over, the canvas drummed taut and shining, the ship went up and down, up and down, and her bowsprit and jibboom clawed as far into the westward and the teeth of the wind as Fox could get her to lie over.

"By God!" he said, to no one in particular. "This is a day to be alive!"

"I daresay, Mr. Fox, you're right." Captain Percy Staunton looked—not green so much as fungoid white —and gripped onto the rail with both hands tightly clenched. He was aware of Fox staring hungrily ahead to where His Britannic Majesty's eighteen-pounder thirty eight gun frigate *Lynx* smashed as they did themselves through the sea, hurling up sheets of spray, her canvas taut, her masts wheeling against the sky. Fox, too, was aware of that look, and could understand

112

Staunton's next remark. The nincompoop, cheery fellow though he was, felt ill and was attempting to display some degree of learning so as partially to cover his weakness.

"It's the damned equinox, Mr. Fox. By thunder, there's always a blow out of the west then."

Fox grunted, and then managed to say: "So it is generally believed, sir. It'll give the Dons a gut-ache —and also it'll give 'em the chance to slip by."

Their stay in Gibraltar had been so short they had not even been given time to go across to Tetuan to water, instead had watered there, a clear indication of the admiral's burning impatience to get them to sea. The westerly had blown up only hours after they had skimmed through the Gut; had it chosen to blow thus foul only slightly earlier they'd still be trapped in the Mediterranean. The two frigates, *Lynx* and *Furieuse* had received very special instructions.

Whilst Fox kept his two good eyes in a minute surveillance of the ship, his mind roved over the extraordinary possibilities the orders received by Captain Staunton might bring to change his whole life.

The war had been going well and not-too well, fortunes of war fluctuating as inevitably they must with two adversaries matched and determined to knock each other out. Spain depended as she had done for centuries on the incredible wealth brought from her South and Central American possessions. The annual flota brought in millions—literally millions—in gold and silver and precious gems.

Should a British sailorman get his hands on some of that loot not only would he be striking a powerful blow for his country, he would assuredly make his fortune. The men would profit by more prize money than all the wages they could earn in a lifetime; for the officers the rewards would be enormous.

113

Somewhere over the western horizon, sailing on from America towards Spain, came the Spanish flota. With it, it brought money that Fox intended to jingle in his pockets.

This was the chance he had prayed for, the kind of chance he had dreamed of. As he knew, carrying the figures in his head, when in 1762 the Spanish treasure ship *Hermione* had been taken off Cadiz, the lieutenants had received £13,000.

Each.

He could feel the rail under his strong bronzed calloused hands. He could feel the wind on his cheek. He could feel the heave and surge of the ship beneath him. He could feel life, free and bold and powerful all around him. And—he could banish all these present feelings and concentrate on the feeling of fat gold pieces trickling through his fingers.

By God! He had to make this chance pay off. Staunton was an admiral's favourite nephew, and yet even that might not be the reason for his despatch on this mission. Captain Stone was the senior officer of these two vessels. They were sailing to join the four frigates waiting for the flota and would prolong the line to the south. The Spanish treasure ships were required to put in at Cadiz; but somehow the idea had grown up that this year they were aiming more northerly, Ferrol or Corunna opposite. Whatever the truth of that Fox found satisfaction in the placing of *Furieuse* in the most southerly position.

Those four frigates with which they were to act in concert were *Naiad*, *Ethalion*, *Triton* and *Alcmene*. Two thirty eights and two thirty twos. Well. *Lynx* and *Furieuse* would add extra bite to the searching line, they could cover a wider arc of sea, make absolutely sure the Spanish flota, however many frigates might be

114

involved this year, were sighted, chased, brought to action, beaten and compelled to strike.

Then—Fox felt the long luxurious shudder ripple through him.

Prize Money! Prize money of such a vast amount he could not hope to think of it rationally.

The equinox had passed some time ago—his own birthday had passed without comment from him or anyone else—and so he had to ignore Staunton's attempt to show sea-lore. In this westerly they'd be hard put to it to handle the Dons; a flying long-bowls kind of shooting match—for once—did not interest Fox. To his great satisfaction the wind moderated as the day wore on and they beat northwards to join the squadron. Fox was inclined these days to be more and more satisfied about quite minor trivialities where, only a few months ago, he would have been a foaming, raging, intolerant black bastard. It must be because he was first lieutenant to a captain with prospects and with the current beautiful prospect of a Spanish treasure flota running down into his broadside.

Ship routine went on as usual. No one, apart from Staunton and Fox, was aware of the reason for their hurried departure from Gibraltar and for this mad tumbling dash. When, on the next day they sighted the squadron, strung out, and were assigned their positions, south of the line, the hands simply went on with their daily routine. Fox knew the officers were seething with excitement, wondering why they were doing what they were doing. He wasn't going to enlighten them. They'd know all they needed to know when the Dons' topsails hove up over the horizon.

The breeze veered, fluctuated, shifted erratically, and then settled down to a moderate north easterly. The line of six frigates, separated by fifteen miles of sea room between each vessel, hunted westwards during the day, and beat back along their latitudes to the east at night. That way, the Spanish would not slip past in the hours of darkness.

October was a month in which the weather could do almost anything it chose, from an Indian summer to howling snowstorms.

On the evening of the fourteenth Fox snuffed the wind and felt it would shift in the night. It would most likely back and die away, and then towards morning get up again with a reasonable briskness—not brisk enough for a reef, of course—from the northwest. He told Parsons to call him and turned in. When Parsons did call him, his intense and permanently worried face creased with concern over the burgoo, Fox sat up and was instantly aware that his prognosis had been correct. The gunroom looked ghostly as he went through. The quarterdeck glimmered palely, everything functioned as it should function; Morgan had the deck. There was the faintest suggestion that Morgan might like to strike up a conversation; a suggestion that Fox quelled instantly by stalking across to the weather side and pacing up and down. One day, and soon, please God! he'd be walking up and down the weather side of his own quarterdeck.

With that shift of wind that Fox with his seaman's bones had snuffed at, the hands were called and the yards swung over so that *Furieuse* kept her dead straight easting. For all his own intemperate demands for a perfection he knew would never be found on any ship, save only the ships that carried dead souls across the bar, Fox saw and heard the quicker tempo of the hands, the way they lay into their tasks.

They had all resented him the moment he'd stepped aboard—all, that, is, with the honourable exceptions of his old Raccoons—and they'd been a lazy crowd, living an easy life with Haining as first of the ship.

116

Well, he'd knocked that idea out of them, and hands to witness punishment had been a not infrequent call piped. Now he could perhaps allow himself the luxury of supposing *Furieuse* was turning into the kind of ship that Captain Sir Cuthbert Rowlands would have cared to command.

That was praise enough for Fox.

Furieuse settled down on her easting, running now with the breeze on her larboard quarter, under easy sail. As soon as the light brightened enough the repeating signal would flutter to *Lynx's* yard-arm and they would turn a full sixteen points and beat back westwards close-hauled on the starboard tack.

Grey came onto the quarterdeck and stood by the larboard mizzen shrouds. Fox was aware of him. The stifling constraints of their relative positions irked Fox and he wondered if that young limb of Satan Mr. Midshipman Lionel Grey shared any of that frustrated feeling. Looking back, Fox saw—and was surprised at the discovery—that Barnabas had the wheel. He had to admit it. Since becoming mixed up with Staunton and all the excitements of a glittering future he had fallen sadly out of touch with his own old hands. And yet—that was normal, perfectly ordinary. As men and officers passed from ship to ship they were shipmates for a time, then they parted.

A hail floated down from the top.

"Deck there!"

Everyone looked up.

The darkness showed streaked with a dun-coloured kind of radiance, warning that the false dawn would soon mock the sea with colour.

"Deck there! There's a sail out there—off the larboard bow, two points—"

Whoever was in the top needed a taste of a starter, Fox told himself, and prepared to bellow savagely,

117

when Morgan, who had the deck, yelled up: "What sail is it?"

"Ship, sir. Can't rightly make her out—"

This was intolerable.

Then, so quickly that it all happened in the space of a half dozen heartbeats, the lookout was yelling frantically, Fox caught the ghostly lattice of dark-grey masts and spars, the faint glimmer of canvas, a lighter grey, and he was roaring out: "Port your helm, Barnabas!" and *Furieuse* was wheeling away and in a rushing smother a large frigate smashed past their larboard bow, their jibboom barely missing the stranger's starboard quarter gallery.

"That's *Lynx!*" Morgan shouted.

"Bloody fool!" yelled Fox. "Wheel amidships, Barnabas!"

Furieuse came back onto her course, her canvas banging like voodoo drums. When the excitement settled down *Lynx* had gone sluicing away to starboard, away to the southeast, and Fox was furiously working out just what scathing comments he would see entered up in the log.

By God! That imbecile Stone had nearly run them down!

Clearly, the shift of wind had taken *Lynx* out of her station and whoever was watch-keeping and whoever had the conn should be dismissed the service.

When dawn came the sea fell to a greasy calmness and the breeze died to a gentle whisper. There was *Lynx,* as bold as brass four miles ahead and to the southeast. With a jolt that he told himself he had no business experiencing at all, Fox heard the lookout sing out: "Sail ho! Broad on the larboard beam!"

Fox knew who that would be, all right. The whole line had come down in the night, or he had drifted north, and he was prepared to back his own sea-keeping qualities against Lemuel Stone's any day.

Lynx was pulling ahead. She was hull down from the deck now. She had a wind, then, that did not reach to *Furieuse*.

"There goes the signal, sir," said Morgan.

They were being signalled, by repeated flag-hoists down the line, to turn to the westward. And then, in that moment, the signal Fox had been waiting for so hungrily.

Grey said without a trace of emotion in his voice: "Sail in sight, sir. Chase to the north."

"Acknowledge," said Fox.

Captain Staunton, rubbing sleep from his eyes, came on deck.

Fox touched his hat.

"They've sighted the Dons, sir. Somewhere to the north. We'll be turning to chase with them."

Staunton stared at Fox.

"Lay me horizontal, Mr. Fox. That's cheery news to run into first thing in the morning!"

Fox wanted to grab the captain's hand and pump it up and down. They were going into a quick action and a swift victory—and then—money! Wealth! Glorious, glorious!

He had no need to take the simple matter of tacking the ship out of Morgan's hands. The watch would change soon, and after breakfast he would send the hands to quarters and have the ship cleared for action. By the good Lord Harry! What a day this was going to be! He could wallow in the sensations of gold pieces, hundreds—no, thousands!—of 'em, trickling and tinkling through his fingers.

Furieuse's hands tumbled on deck as the pipes twittered.

Fox looked aloft. He'd have the royals out, bigod

he would! He'd run this leaky old sieve of a ship, no matter how beautiful she looked to the casual outside eye, he'd run her bows under to get at the Dons.

He said to Midshipman O'Leary, a pimply boy with buck teeth: "Pass the word for Wilson. Have him go up to the crosstrees."

"Aye aye, sir," squeaked O'Leary, and scampered off to find a bosun's mate to pass the word along.

Fox felt more comfortable with Wilson on lookout. Wilson was reputed to have the sharpest eyes in the fleet. And there were very few ships he could not identify from a pocket handkerchief-sized scrap of sail just above the horizon rim.

Presently Wilson called down: "*Deck there*! There's a second sail with *Lynx*!"

Fox's first thought was that Stone had come up with a treasure frigate all on his own. If he ran out of sight then Toady Stone would have all the prize money to himself. But the hunting line of four frigates to the north had signaled the treasure ships as being to the north. Then how was it that Stone had run into one of them to the southeast? Fox had had the signal strung out for *Lynx;* but had had no reply.

Wilson yelled again: "She's a liner, sir. A seventy four—French."

"Oh My God!" said Fox, and saw it all, and was appalled.

He thought of all that was at stake. The fat money-laden Spanish frigates were over the horizon to the north. There were four British frigates somewhere about to go in chase of them in a chase that might last all day and well into the night until they came up with them and brought them to action. If *Furieuse* was not within sight of the action she could claim not a penny prize money. He thought of his family of Foxes by the Thames, his mother and brothers and sisters who depended on him for their livelihood. He thought of Toady Stone, and what he owed that unspeakable man, and how he would joy—had intended to gloat—in thus turning away to the north and leaving Stone to run over the horizon going the wrong way and being far too late in discovering his mistake.

He thought of the responsibility he owed his family and when Morgan, Staunton, the others who had come onto the quarterdeck, looked at him, he looked firmly back at Morgan and stuck his hands into the small of his back, and said nothing.

Let Stone stew!

He was not the captain of *Furieuse,* was Fox, but he was in a position tantamount to command. His position was very familiar to many first lieutenants in the navy, not so many now, true, as in the old days. Some very well known and well-connected gentlemen fancied themselves in the blue coat and cocked hat of a captain or an admiral. They made sure their commands stayed mighty close to Chatham so that they might get up to London whenever the mood took them. The Master and the first lieutenant ran the ship. At the first whisper of blue sea and gunsmoke they favoured their gout and retired to Bath or Cheltenham or Tunbridge Wells.

Let Toady Stone reap the full benefits of his villainy!

Wilson hallooed again.

"Gunsmoke, sir. The Froggy's engaging *Lynx*, sir!"

With this wind the sullen booming of the great guns would not roll up. But Wilson could see. And so could the rest of the ship's company. They knew the score now. A British frigate was being attacked by a French seventy four, and they were running away. No other explanation could be conceived.

They could see.

121

But George Abercrombie Fox could not.

Both his eyes abruptly coated over with blue-purple linings like the Duke of Hell's cloak.

By the feel of the wind on his face he could orient himself, and by the feel of the ship beneath him he could orient the ship. He dared not let go of the rail.

Toady Stone—another five minutes and the lubber would have been below the horizon, and then he could have been smashed up and sunk by the French seventy four without Fox knowing a thing about it. He'd sent Wilson up so as to see the Spanish treasure frigates early; Wilson had simply brought this problem to him.

He heard Staunton clear his throat.

"Ah, Mr. Fox—Captain Stone—ah, *Lynx*—"

At least he wasn't saddled with a captain who thought he knew how to run a ship. Percy Staunton would do as Fox said. But—after that? And, already he had seen Percy in different colours; perhaps the admiral's nephew would not submit thus tamely to being told to run away from a Frenchy.

Fox could imagine the ring of faces of the officers on the quarterdeck. Their eyes would be burning into him. They would be weighing, remembering. They didn't like him; they'd report unfavorably when the story got out.

But—his family. And all that gold!

The old forgotten wound that made his left eye, and sometimes his right, lose all vision with that damned ring of purple and black in moments of action or danger or lust had served him ill before. But now—he could brazen it out. He could. The orders were to sail to the north for the Spanish flota. But, down there in the southeast a British thirty eight fought a French seventy four. There was, really, only one

122

thing he could order. He would order it not out of patriotic fervour, but only to stop from being broken.

"Put the ship about," said Fox. "We'll teach that Frog!"

CHAPTER TWELVE

Everything was ready.

Chains lashed the yards to the masts. Extra preventer stays had been fixed. The decks had been sanded. All the captain's furniture had been carried below. The gunner was down in the magazine ready to supervise the handling of the cartridges, and the ship's boys were waiting ready to begin their mad scampering with their leather buckets of cartridge. The galley fire had been doused. The men stood to their guns silently. The marines had taken up their positions. Staunton had shifted into a full dress uniform, and looked a perfect peacock. Fox wore his oldest kit. He'd had enough of fine new uniforms being ruined in battle, and to hell with the glory and traditions of battle.

The Purser would have to tackle the wounded down on the after cockpit, with the midshipmen's sea chests thrust together to make an operating table.

The guns had been cast off, the port lids triced up, the weapons drawn and reloaded, and run out. Now *Furieuse* sliced through the sea towards *Lynx* and the Frenchman and now they could hear the distant rolling thunder of the broadsides.

That made Fox grimace.

Toady Stone had no business putting his frigate into the position where the Frogs could fire a broadside at her at all.

In his drawing-up of the watch-keeping bill and his working out of the quarter stations, Fox had indulged himself and, with Grey acting as signal midshipman, had placed Carker in command of four of the carronades on the quarterdeck. Master's Mate Andrew Williamson and Midshipman Simpson commanded the remainder, under Dillon. Down on the upper deck Haining and Morgan commanded the main battery of eighteen pounders. Fox had not forgotten his first impressions of Smythe, the Marine lieutenant. He had had no warrant to suppose the man shy and would not have thought it possible, his own feelings about the marines being based on their unfailing courage and gallantry in action. It was, therefore, a comfort to know that Sergeant Cartwright was on hand if needs be.

And, as Fox thus sailed down to engage his frigate in battle with a seventy four to rescue a deadly foe, the wealth of Croesus slipped away beyond the farther horizon.

The irony of it all did not please George Abercrombie Fox one whit.

Allied to his love of Molière was his love of François Villon. His regret had been keen that Don Salvator had possessed no Villon in his library. Fox rather felt that the sad scent of lost opportunities and wasted time of which Villon sang so beautifully fitted the present situation well. But, then, Jean Baptiste Poquelin had all that off to perfection with a laugh and a giggle at man's pretensions.

Down on the upper deck Morgan and Haining were deep in conversation, and Fox guessed they were discussing women, or race horses, or the gun-room wine bill—anything except the seventy four iron-lipped guns towards which they sailed.

Men thought of funny things at times like these; Fox knew of very little better than Molière. But, with a captain who left everything to him to do—sensible man—Fox now concentrated his mind on the coming battle.

Furieuse was going at seven knots and she appeared to be finding nothing of the wind that had whipped *Lynx* to the southeast. If the breeze died and they were within range of the Frenchman—it would be goodbye *Furieuse*.

The gunfire brisked and Staunton, chuckling, his Adam's Apple gobbling, said: "A damned fine day for a fight, eh, Mr. Fox?"

"Any day's a good day for a fight," said Fox. "Provided you can kick the other guy in the guts first."

By this time Percy had a better understanding of his first lieutenant, so he could chuckle and rub his hands together, and burble: "Dashed if that ain't sound advice, Mr. Fox, trice me up if it ain't."

Fox walked forward and jumped up into the lee main shrouds. He climbed up a few ratlines and peered, balancing his telescope easily with the motion of the ship.

Out of the cloud bank of gunsmoke the masts of the ships rose, naked of canvas but trailing gay bunting. There were six masts, so no one had yet struck a decisive blow that would make steering difficult if not impossible for the opponent. From the way they were lying, it looked as though they were grappled; the three tall masts of the seventy four lay slightly forward and astraddle the three masts of *Lynx*. Smoke continued to belch upwards and to roll gently away downwind. Fox looked. His eyes, after that complete failure when he was faced with a decision he knew would take the bread out of the mouths of his family for the sake of a man he would as lief stick in the belly, were now functioning perfectly.

He must keep the weather gage. There would be no breaking past the Frenchman and luffing up under his lee to compel him to fight. The seventy four would be only too anxious to get a British frigate under his guns. Mind you, with two frigates . . . H'mm. Perhaps there might be the chance of frightening the Frog off, and then of beating back like the clappers to get at the Dons . . . He might have his cake and eat it . . .

Wilson yelled: "Deck there! Another Frenchy! A sloop! She's beating up to the liner!"

Fox did not take his hat off and jump on it. He climbed sedately back down the ratlines, jumped onto the quarterdeck, tucked his telescope under his arm, and paced deliberately across to Captain Staunton.

He was aware that every eye fastened upon him.

He could say goodbye to a quick action and a go at the Dons.

He was cursing away under his breath in a manner that would have frizzled Staunton's ears could he have heard it first.

"Yes, Mr. Fox?"

Fox reminded himself that he had rescued this dashing young ignoramus of a captain from the clutches of a score or so of gunboats who had shot his command to pieces and sunk her. Just how Staunton—or Greaves, his first—had got into that position, Fox had felt it tactful not to enquire. But no harm would be done if he explained to Percy just what it was he was getting into.

Fox drew Staunton away out of earshot of the others on the quarterdeck.

"We would have danced around the seventy four and shot her up, raked her, bashed in her stern-galleries, made her sorry she'd grappled *Lynx*. But now, while we are doing that, that pesky corvette is going to do the same for us."

"I see, Mr. Fox. By Jove! That sounds unhealthy, don't you know."

127

"Unhealthy," said Fox. "Aye, mighty unhealthy."

"So what's the jolly old order of the day, then, Mr. Fox?"

How dearly Fox would have liked to reply: "You're the captain, you give the orders." But; Staunton had never professed to be a ship captain, or to take advantage of his position. To give him his due, he had always played fair with Fox. And, always, there hovered the formidable figure of his uncle, Admiral Staunton, in the background.

"We will let the Frogs see our teeth, sir, and then we'll backheel, as it were, and scupper the corvette."

"Capital, Mr. Fox, capital."

Percy Staunton chuckled as though it was already accomplished.

At each gun stood its crew, ready to slave at their divine service of their iron idol. In each crew stood the fireman, with bucket handy, the sail trimmer, who could be called away to sail-haul if necessary, the boarder with his cutlass and pistol. Yes, he had a crew who, if they were not moulded as he liked, would damned-well fight. He thought of Ponty, left ashore at Gibraltar, and wished he had not lost the Dane, for they were bonny fighters, like the Swedes, of which nationality there were at least ten in his crew. Joachim, the gunner's mate, was a German. Slattery was an American. The Americans were really English—or British—and they'd fight like maniacs. The Lithuanian, the Pole, the five Italians, the two Russians—well, they were a mixed bag to be sailing down to fight Monsieur Johnny Crapaud.

Up on the quarterdeck and among the crew manning one of Grey's carrondades stood Abdul, the giant black they had acquired from the Turks. He had been stationed there so that, should the helmsmen be shot down, he might leap to the wheel and take over. Always supposing, Fox thought with a sour bile, there was any wheel left to man.

Furieuse soared on over the sea, all her canvas drawing, urging her on to what might prove her destruction.

The seventy four would have thirty six pounders on the lower deck; twelves or eighteens on the upper, and she'd mount some of those brass thirty six pounder carronades on her quarterdeck. A full broadside would take *Furieuse* and lift her by the scruff of the neck and toss her aside, her back broken, to crumple and collapse and slide beneath the waves.

What the hell Stone was doing with *Lynx* in the impossible situation he placed her in, Fox didn't know.

Little time had elapsed since he had given the order to go about and the frigate slid towards the action as the sound of gunfire increased. Fox worked out vectors and angles in his mind, and took what crumb of comfort he could from that.

Now they could see the two ships ahead. *Lynx* had managed to shift herself away from any immediate blasting effects of the Frenchman's broadside; but although she had managed to position herself athwart the seventy four's bows, she was herself almost quarter on, and could bring to bear only the last few of her eighteen pounders and quarterdeck carronades.

For a moment the sound of gunfire slackened. The smoke drifted to leeward. Coming down from to windward as he was, Fox had the options of position.

He walked towards Barnabas at the wheel. He had already done a long trick. Ben Ferris was with him. The helmsman's position on a frigate like this was exposed, there was no poop to shelter him. The timoneer stood perilously in danger.

"Barnabas. And you too, Ben. We're going down under the Frog's counter. We'll boot him in the arse

129

as we go, then we'll come about smartly, and give him the starboard side. Make it smart."

"Aye aye, sir," said Barnabas, and "Aye aye, sir," said Ben Ferris. Raccoons both. But, Fox corrected himself crossly, Furry-arses, both.

He went back to the quarterdeck rail.

Staunton was hopping up and down from one foot to the other. Grey stood quite patiently. There would be no damn signals made for a time yet; and when the need came they might have no yards or masts left from which to hang the flags. But, in all conscience, he could not order Grey off the quarterdeck. And— Grey had every right to be here. This was how young gentlemen learned the trade of sea-butchery for King George.

This Frog ahead, now, would provide a suitable chopping block. He'd probably slipped out and evaded the blockade during a time when the British had been blown off station, and there was no disgrace in that to a man like Fox who knew all about the perils, the monotony and the technical expertise of maintaining a continuous close-blockade. There might be others. This lone seventy four and her attendant corvette might be merely an outlier of a whole squadron of Frenchmen. There might be eighties and eighty fours, first-rate three-deckers, a whole Fleet might be out. Then Fox brushed aside these wild speculations. He had one ship of the line to deal with. She had spotted a lone British frigate and had pounced, like a terrier seeking to snap a rat's back between his jaws. Well, Fox was bringing up a second rat; between them they had to castrate the terrier and then get to hell out of it.

Grey called: *"Lynx's* mizzen has gone, sir."

"Thank you, Mr. Grey." Staunton spoke with per-fect protocol, as though accustomed to sailing into

130

battle on his own quarterdeck. Well; he'd done it once before, to Fox's sure knowledge.

Now *Lynx* would be hard set to manoeuvre out of harm's way.

Wilson yelled down from the masthead.

"*Deck there*! The sloop's spotted us, sir. She's bearing up."

Staunton cocked an eye at Fox. Fox kept his ugly face composed. His brain went over his calculations again, adjusting. He said: "If the sloop's foolish enough to engage us before we hit the seventy four, he's only himself to blame."

The time which although measurable in minutes had passed as slowly as a hay wain trundling home at dusk, now shot forward like a po'chaise taking bloods to London. The smoke and confusion of the fight leaped towards them across the tumbled blue sea. The concussions of gunfire which had slacked now broke out again. The sloop—she looked incredibly beautiful, leaning over, all her canvas taut, spray sheeting—hurtled towards them.

Fox worked out the angles. He kept his whole point of aim fixed on the seventy four's stern. If the corvette crossed his course, she would suffer. He would ignore her until he had dealt that first vital broadside right up the Frog's backside.

Furieuse skipped over the sea. *Lynx's* fore-topmast fell overside. Now, if Stone was not rescued, he was done for.

He leaned over the quarterdeck rail.

"Mr. Haining! Have your sail trimmers ready. I want to go about instantly."

"Aye aye, sir," shouted back Haining.

Fox felt mild surprise that he had given his orders in such a mild tone, without bluster. He bethought himself of what a captain was expected to do, and

131

turning to Staunton said in a low voice: "Perhaps you would care to speak a few words to the hands, sir?"

Percy brightened. His bright eyes and chinless face and bobbing Adam's Apple all came together in a macabre good-natured mask of ferocity. He told the hands what they wanted to hear, good rousing fustian stuff, with plenty of rum and flogging and good King George and Corsican bandits, and honour of the flag and the country. Fox thought of the Spanish prize money drawing further and further away over the northern horizon.

But, think those sour thoughts though he might, he was watching the two ships ahead and he saw the way the puffs of wind were swinging them. If those puffs failed altogether . . . He wouldn't contemplate that; the corvette was bringing a fine wind and she was sheering off, clearly unwilling to take on this big burly frigate single-handed. Fox gave a few course-adjustment orders and *Furieuse* settled down so that, according to Fox's calculations, she would pass a pistol shot distance past the seventy four's stern.

Pistol shot was usually reckoned to be fifty yards. Musket shot at three hundred yards. Fox intended to discharge his larboard broadside of one twelve, thirteen eighteens, and seven thirty two's directly into the gilded and windowed stern of the Frenchman. At fifty yards the destruction should be decisive.

"Fire as she bears!" he yelled down. "There's a flogging for every gun captain who fires early—and his crew."

They all knew this was no idle threat.

Now the sea distance narrowed with fantastic speed. The corvette had come about and was hanging off their starboard quarter. Any minutes now her ten larboard nine pounders would belch a broadside that might cut a vital line aboard *Furieuse,* bring her up unmanageably under the guns of the seventy four.

To hell with the corvette! Get on! Get on!

Furieuse roared down on the ship of the line. Both Fox's eyes were working perfectly. He was aware of Staunton gulping and gripping his sword hilt. The corvette fired. The shot whined and moaned above. A halliard parted with a twang. A round black hole appeared in the mizzen topsail. *Furieuse's* bowsprit reached past the seventy four's stern.

Now!

The frigate's broadside began firing from the bow.

CHAPTER THIRTEEN

"Glorious! Glorious!" sang out Captain Staunton.

"Splendid!" said old Burlington, the Master.

Dillon was hopping with impatience to get his carronades into action.

The blattering smacking of the eighteen pounders belched in a gouting line of smoke down *Furieuse's* deck as she glided past the Frenchman's stern. That smoke was caught and hurled away leeward by the flukey wind. Fox stood by the rail and stared at the ship of the line and said not a word.

He saw the brilliant gilt gingerbread work shredded. He saw two of the lanterns explode like those hog's bladders of water men shied at at fairs. He saw the broad sweep of stern galleries and windows smashed and thrust inwards as though a drunk stuck his fist through a boozer's window. He saw the splintering of timbers on the gun-deck level. He saw a great wedge-shaped piece go flying off the rudder as though some demented child had bitten a piece of cake and spat it out. He saw all this before the smoke blotted everything in a grey and brown pall of odiferous blindness.

Also, he saw the name of the seventy four, blazoned all across her stern. The name of this French National ship of the line was *Zodiaque*. A second later Dillon's carronades fired and the letters 'que' were instantly swept away. Fox looked, as the smoke choked down, and read, and pondered.

"And you, too," said G. A. Fox, turning with equanimity upon the quarterdeck to roust out the crew of a carronade who were tripping over themselves in their eagerness to reload.

He rather liked that little diversion in the smoke of battle.

The truth was, all the fire and fury had been unleashed from the British frigate, and poor *Zodiaque* had taken a severe knock. Mind you—this was the way a cautious commander tried always to bring his ship into action. Fox remembered *Mortagne* and many other fine vessels that had been smitten with their death blows thus early in the fight.

Lynx was a mess.

She had lost all her masts now, and a horrible raffle of wreckage tangled drifting alongside. Smoke obscured much of her; but marines were firing from her waist and quarterdeck, and no doubt the French had made some attempt to board. *Zodiaque* towered in the smoke. All her masts still stood, although she had lost her main-topgallant, and much of her canvas and rigging hung shredded down. Fox frowned. *Furieuse* was coming about as he had ordered, for Haining had taken care of that evolution with a punctilio driven by Fox's express orders; but the hanging canvas of *Zodiaque* indicated the flukey nature of the breeze. If *Furieuse* lost the wind, there'd be hell to pay.

Furieuse surged back and her starboard broadside thunked out, Morgan walking swiftly down the deck to control each eighteen pounder, and, as he disappeared under the quarterdeck, so Dillon took up the discharges with his carronades.

Twice! Two almighty kicks up the backside.

Just what *Zodiaque's* gun decks were like now Fox could only too-well imagine. He had been in a ship that had been raked. He could personally vouch that

135

the experience was unpleasant; one of the most unpleasant known to man. But he was not looking at *Zodiaque*. He leaned out and looked forward, a few points off *Furieuse's* larboard bow. Yes! There was the corvette, swinging around daintily and as he looked so her ten nine pounders let fly. That familiar nauseating shattering crash reached him from forward. One at least of the corvette's shot had found a mark. On the instant a spattering of blocks erupted from under the foretop—double-blocks for the spritsail brace, the leech line and the buntlines, and four single blocks for the spritsail topsail brace. The whole edifice of canvas on the foremast convulsed. Before the blocks had time to bounce on the deck Fox was roaring in a furious volley of filthy oaths. Sneyd the bosun and his mates with such of the hands as could be spared raced aloft to patch up the damage. The head of *Furieuse* swung waveringly to starboard. She'd be in irons in a flash if Fox failed to react correctly. He snarled the orders to Barnabas and to Dillon, and the driver eased over with the helm, loosening the frigate through the water.

A pole—it was Jeczmyk, called, inevitably, Jammy by the crew—had received a nine inch block in his head. His torso was thrown overboard.

Confusion boiled. Then Fox had her in hand again and could with what canvas he had wheel her around to tear in once more. As they surged past the corvette Fox watched with some satisfaction as the broadside lashed out. The corvette's main mast buckled into the shape of the letter Z—main, top and top-gallant masts all at crazy angles—and collapsed, the canvas ballooning and plopping into her wash.

That was the corvette out of the reckoning.

But the captain of the seventy four had his wits about him. No doubt he was driving on a half-trained crew who, although brave enough, lacked the sea-experience that could sustain them through a prolonged action. *Zodiaque* had pushed off from *Lynx* and her head was swinging. She had been badly smashed about; she was freeing herself of her helpless antagonist so as to be clear for a deadly broadside at her new opponent.

Fox was as well aware as the next man that there was a doubt, a serious doubt, that the French sailors would stand to their guns past the time when ordinary mortal men would give in and refuse once again to sponge and load and ram and run-out and fire. That the British sailors did this was merely a testimonial to their training and to the determination of their officers, applied in the form of brutal discipline. The French were no less courageous than the British; they just worked from different principles—principles which Fox, as a human being, shared; but which Fox, as a British Naval Officer, could only view with rejection.

In this game the stick won out over the carrot.

Which was a bestial thought and one he had no time for now, not with *Zodiaque* continuing her swing so that all her doubledecked broadside moved solidly around to bear on the British frigate. Fox yelled helm orders and Barnabas crabbed *Furieuse* away. Fox wouldn't run in yard arm to yard arm—not against fourteen thirty sixes, fifteen eighteens, and eight thirty six pounder carronades—plus whatever she carried on her forecastle. He eyed the sky with a black feeling of anger. Goddam wind! It was more flukey than ever, and *Zodiaque's* captain was taking full advantage of his opportunity to face up to his oponent. Still—Fox had the fleeter ship under him, the nimbler, a swift saucy frigate that should run rings around the big lumbering ship of the line. That it did not always work out like that could not be allowed to deflect him.

Lynx was out of it, a dismasted shambles.

Furieuse bore in, luffed-up shot past *Zodiaque's* quarter.

Her broadside lashed out. Still no spars fell aboard the Frenchman, and Fox cursed luridly.

They came about, creaming through the sea, and the wind died and their canvas flapped dolefully. With still a hint of the breeze *Zodiaque* bore to cross their bows. She'd rake them!

She would!

Fox looked at Staunton, who stared ahead, his pop-eyes glazed. Everyone could see the slow and inexorable onward movement of the liner from their larboard bow across their stem. In only moments she would disappear beneath the leaping billows of smoke; and all hell would break out on the frigate.

Fox felt a puff of wind stir against his cheek.

He bellowed, the hands ran to haul, the ship's head came slowly around, tracking the head of *Zodiaque*. Now the ships lay at forty five degrees, with their bowsprits a musket shot apart. He daren't wait much longer. As soon as the guns bore. They could be hand-spiked around so as to fire obliquely and Fox had private theories as to how he might achieve at least two points and possibly three points of traverse. As it was he felt reasonably happy about this heavy degree of training because he had personally inspected every breeching of every gun. Tremendous and unequal strains came onto the breeching if the gun was not fired directly on the broadside. He just hoped no one else was going to be killed or maimed, as poor Ponty had been, by a runaway gun.

Without a word to Staunton, Fox ran down off the quarterdeck and hared along the upper deck. He came up to the forward eighteen pounder. Mr. Midshipman Gruber was squeaking out to his crew to: "Spike her around, you great whoreson lubbers!"

138

Shocking language these babies picked up, to be sure.

Fox watched as Grimes, a seaman with red hair and a squint, heaved his handspike around. The eighteen pounder traversed. Then Fox peered along the line of metal. Yes; in two more minutes the gun would bear. He ran back with a shout to Gruber: "Keep 'em at it, Mr. Gruber."

"Aye aye, sir!" came back the excited squeak.

Fox reached the quarterdeck, having checked the alignment of the guns, and then the eighteen pounders began to fire, a rippled concussion down the deck. Smoke blew and shredded away, clear indication the breeze was freshening. *Zodiaque* without the training of the British ship could not train her guns sufficiently; *Furieuse* got off two full broadsides before Fox saw the gouts of smoke leap ominously from the two-decker's side.

"For what we are about to receive," the words ghosted up in his mind, "may the Lord make us truly thankful."

Then the roundshot struck.

Dillon was splattered all across the deck, a red smear.

The maintopgallant swayed and toppled and crashed down in a spattering of tackle and lethal blocks and torn canvas.

The deck rang by the larboard quarterdeck rail and a savage gouge appeared miraculously across the planking.

The mizzenmast bitts disappeared into flying chips.

Three men of the carronade crew right next to Fox screamed and staggered back, jagged splinters of oak spearing their contorted bodies.

Blood stank into the air, mingling with the stink of gun smoke. Midshipman Callaghan was staring at his left wrist, pumping blood; where the hand was God knew. Lestock, the big stroke of the captain's barge, was sinking to his knees, a splinter two-feet long like some obscene tentacle protruding from his back. Mr. Burlington, the Master, took his hat off and looked curiously at its brim, which was jagged and torn as though savaged by a wolfhound.

"Keep 'em at it, Mr. Haining!" screamed Fox.

"Aye aye, sir!" roared back Morgan. He stared up, his face already powder-blacked, his eyes like coals. "Mr. Haining is cut in two, sir."

"Traverse onto the broadside!" Fox screeched his orders. He had to work the ship now, as well as plan her manoeuvres. He got her around, drew away from *Zodiaque*. They endured another broadside with its consequent damage. An eighteen pounder sprang muzzle-up, twisting, booming like a gong, toppled full across Rawlinson and Callaghan. More blocks and tackle rained down from aloft. The mizzen topgallant split and flew out like a tattered flag.

Then they were past and Fox was roaring Sneyd onto the most urgent repairs so as to bring the ship around and once more thrust her into the devil's inferno.

"Warm work, Mr. Fox." Staunton was positively glowing.

"Aye, sir. And warmer yet if they don't run."

Very wisely, Staunton said: "The Frogs can't know we're a crack ship, Mr. Fox. They must still believe a seventy four can whip us."

Fox did not say: "God help you." When you looked at it, Staunton was a fair plucked 'un.

He said: "The Dons will be glad of *Zodiaque*, though."

"Money," said Staunton. "All the money in the
140

world can't buy the glory we're winning today, Mr. Fox."

There was no answer to that. At least, no answer that Fox could make. *Furieuse* stood in again. There was no getting out of it now. The butcher's bill would have to be paid. Until this thumping two-decker was crippled, until he brought a mast down, Fox daren't leave her to swing north and interfere with the four frigates engaged with the flota. That was what this was all about now. It had begun with his reluctant rescue of Toady Stone; it had now become his duty to keep this big adversary away from the plans of their Lords of the Admiralty.

Once more they plunged in and once more the roundshot and the grape scythed across their decks. Midshipman Simpson and master's mate Williamson went down at the carronades.

Fox roared at Carker: "They're all yours now, Mr. Carker. Keep 'em fighting."

"Aye aye, sir," shouted Carker, in his usual way, phlegmatic, concerned only that he do his duty in the best possible way he could.

Midshipman Gruber was on the quarterdeck, his face a black mask, his hand to his mouth from which blood dribbled. When he spoke Fox had trouble hearing.

"Pleathe, thir, Mithter Morganth dead."

Fox gripped Gruber's narrow shoulder.

"Go below, Mr. Gruber, and have that mouth seen to." He pushed the boy away. Now he yelled with ferocious black anger. "Mr. Grey! You'll oblige me by taking command of the main battery." He glared as Grey came up, wearing that familiar quizzical look that looked through and through the coarse tarpaulin Lieutenant Fox. "Keep 'em at it, Mr. Grey."

"Aye aye, sir."

141

And Grey swung off, jumping very athletically and nonchalantly down the quarterdeck ladder to the upper deck.

"We're losing a lot o' good men, Mr. Fox."

"Yes." Fox eyed Staunton. For all the good he was doing he might as well have been rowing in Plymouth Sound. But Fox knew the breed; much as he detested almost all of them. Staunton wouldn't be anywhere else for a fortune.

Furieuse came in again and this time Fox brought her cunningly against *Zodiaque's* bows. Grey's efforts with the guns on the upper deck and Carker's with those on the quarterdeck bore bloody fruit. The smoke gushed and the concussions tore and battered at the eardrums, the world filled with the wildly exciting smell of cannon-smoke.

"It's going!" someone yelled.

Fox cocked an evil eye.

Zodiaque's fore-topmast swayed, lines parted, the sail bulged, then the whole top-hamper swooped down. As it splashed into the sea the two-decker fired and flaming wads ignited the canvas. Fox could see the dark agitated figures of men racing out onto her fore castle, over the cathead, pushing and hurling buckets of water. He saw gold lace wink on the shoulders of a man wielding an axe.

"Sarn't Cartwright!" he bellowed. "Clear that party off there, if you please, double quick!"

If Cartwright answered, Fox didn't hear; but presently the marine's fire cleared the forecastle. The blaze died down, however, and Fox cursed. That had been a chance to set the seventy four ablaze, and he had muffed it. Confound it! As his thoughts tumbled pell-mell through his head *Furieuse* shuddered to the fresh impacts of the next broadside.

They couldn't last long like this. The two-decker

142

would be difficult to manoeuvre without the leverage of her foretop sail, damned difficult. He ought to lie up under the quarter and blast her out of the water. But she'd have a big crew, better than six hundred men, nearer seven hundred. Once they were given the chance of boarding it would be touch and go, even allowing for a couple of hundred dead out of the total.

He brought *Furieuse* about again in the smoke.

He made up his mind to hold *Furieuse* on the lee quarter of *Zodiaque,* and shoot until he had to shift as she sagged down on him. He could manage that. There were far too many dead men cumbering the decks. Marines were carrying a wounded comrade below. He yelled and men sprang in this brief interlude to hurl their messmates overboard. The mangled bodies splashed unheard into the wake.

At three or four places on the two-decker's sides the dark stain of blood showed trickling down from the scuppers.

Whoever her captain was, he was earning Fox's respect. By the time the frigate came about again for another pass, this time with the difference that Fox intended to haul up under the two-decker's squarter, the French already had a spar hoisted as a jury-rigged foretopmast and were slinging a yard across. Fox would like to meet that Frog captain. He was a fighter.

Fox had not forgotten those two slogging blows he had delivered in the very first moments of his battle, blows that should have crippled the seventy four; and she'd been fighting *Lynx* before that.

Thought of their consort made him seek her out through the flat wreaths of smoke. She just lay in the water, a dismasted hulk, helpless. The sloop lay beyond her, and a sketchy kind of mainmast was rising amidships. Fox curled his lips in his evil smile. He'd pay that sloop a visit shortly; that would give his men a break and the satisfaction of seeing the results of their handiwork. With *Zodiaque*, now, the big lumbering seventy four looked very little different from when they'd begun.

Even as he looked a jury-rigged foremast began to lift aboard *Lynx*. So someone—if Toady Stone was dead—was working in her. Fox wasn't sure if he would welcome Stone's death in this fashion.

Zodiaque swung as he came in again, foiling his first attempt to put his sails to the mast on her lee quarter. He went on past, blasting with all the guns and carronades Grey and Carker could bring to bear. The smoke jetted. Men shrieked and died as the return fire came in; the mainmast shuddered. Looking with a horror that was all for the ship, Fox saw a gigantic chunk gouged from the mainmast, six feet from the deck level, a chunk ten inches through and two feet high. Hell! He daren't ask the timbers to take the kinds of strain he usually called for; the mast would snap and splinter for a certainty.

This time, gingerly, Fox swore.

When *Furieuse* foamed back with the wind brisking and the smoke dissipating leewards, *Zodiaque* showed her full broadside and Fox was not prepared to subject his sorely battered ship to that devilish punishment once more. His voice rapped like a leaden guinea. "Ease her, Barnabas."

He let her head fall off. The main course was clewed up; he daren't put that kind of strain on the mainmast. Mr. O'Hare came up and knuckled his forehead and said: "Three feet in the well, sir."

"Thank you, Mr. O'Hare."

"It's making, sir; but I can hold it if we don't get any more 'twixt win and water."

"I expect we shall, Mr. O'Hare."

144

"Aye aye, sir."

O'Hare went off. Amazing, really, how men behaved in action.

Fox had actually to recollect himself.

"Mr. O'Hare! Look at the mainmast! Get that seen to at once." Fox gave quick instructions involving fishing and splicing and taking he didn't care what timbers from he didn't care where. O'Hare would patch the mast somehow; but that maincourse wouldn't be set this side of Plymouth.

The main hatchway had been smashed as though a gigantic scraper had been drawn across it, the coamings splintered down level with the deck planking. The bitts were in pieces and the belaying points of sheets and braces were everywhere hitched to whatever was handy. He thought that this would prove Sneyd's fitness to be a boatswain one way or the other, if the man was not killed. Too many men had been killed. And still *Zodiaque* awaited their next pass.

No, bigod! She was turning, was swinging, was filling her canvas and bearing down on them.

Fox's gargoyle face remained graven. He would not turn tail—he couldn't do that—but he could take evasive measures and seek to use his last card. He still thought the frigate more manoeuvrable. He would put that card to the test.

Staunton said: "*Lynx* has a jury mainmast, Mr. Fox."

"We've got to do this on our own."

"Oh—of course! Lay me horizontal, Mr. Fox, if I thought else?" Staunton clutched his sword. "D'ye think, Mr. Fox, we might board her? Damned Froggies, smashing up my lovely ship. I'd dearly love to board 'em and teach 'em manners."

"If we have to board, Captain Staunton, I think the men will follow most bravely."

145

Staunton stared at him. "Well, of course they will, Mr. Fox! Damned queer thing to say, my oath on't."

Fox turned away. The two vessels approached each other, stem to stem. Fox knew now he was not facing the normal run of French sea captain. This man would hold on. If the two-decker struck the frigate it wouldn't be the Frenchman who would suffer worst from the collision. Fox would have to turn away. He worked out the angles, blistered his orders, *Furieuse* came around gently and then once more the blasting succession of shocks burst out. In the smoke with the guns leaping on their trucks and the hideous sound of roundshot blustering past, the click and snap of musket balls, the pinging of parting rigging, *Furieuse* put in her broadsides—three to the French two—and roared on. More blood stained her planking, more dead men were thrown overboard, more maimed men were carried below.

Fox wore carefully. The Frenchman wore, also— he was in no better condition to tack than Fox—but Fox detected a hanging in the evolution. *Zodiaque* did not come fully around.

Fox saw his chance.

Under his intemperate tongue with its strings of foul sea oaths the hands brought *Furieuse* up and over, the sea foaming past, all the rigging thrumming under the extra strains. He saw the foremast, which was the only mast aboard that should be upright and unraked, leaning forward. He damned it to perdition. This was his chance and he wasn't going to miss it now.

The frigate heaved and groaned as she slid through the sea. The men stood to their guns. The two-decker loomed above them, enormous, her masts raking into the air. Fox walked back to Barnabas and Ben Ferris. They were aware of his presence. The ship held her

146

course like a canal narrow-boat, dead straight down a beam-wide cut. *Zodiaque's* captain saw what Fox was up to and the seventy four's yards went over.

"Too late, you bastard!" said Fox.

Now they were fairly up to the seventy four's quarter. They were roaring past under her stern.

"This time," shouted Fox. "This time you've got to knock away more than a single damned spar!"

His men cheered. Bloody fools. They bent to their red hot guns. Carker and Grey walked among them, quiet, calm, yet fired by the same kind of manic excitement that Fox himself suppressed so well.

Now!

The broadside thundered, gun answering gun, and the carronades taking up the belching roar of smoke and iron.

What was happening aboard *Zodiaque* now gave Fox twin emotions. One of infinite regret that good men were being killed and maimed. And the other of a fierce and altogether primitive exultation that he was smashing his enemy into bloody ruin.

Furieuse ran on and *Zodiaque* swung away. "Come about!" shrieked Fox and in that instant his whole foremast swayed, gave a wriggle like a snake, and collapsed in smothering ruin.

Ruin!

Complete and absolute.

Long before he could clear the raffle and rig a jury foremast the two-decker would be around and broadside on to his stern and would pound him into bloodied wreckage.

He stared with passionate intensity at the Frenchman and she vanished from his sight as that bloody ring of purple and black with the pink flying spots closed down like the fist of some torturer of the Inquisition.

147

He just stood there, dazed, fully comprehending the disaster, hearing the yells and screams, the rush of naked feet on the deck, the clattering clang and rending scrape of the fallen spars.

Staunton was screaming in his ear.

She's turning away, Mr. Fox! She's running! *She's running*!"

As though he had wiped a hand across a frosted window pane, Fox could see again.

Zodiaque had filled and was bearing away, running full and bye, all the canvas her masts would hold drawing. She was spreading her wings and leaving them. And they a wallowing hulk in the water! *Zodiaque* was flying for Cadiz.

Very slowly Fox turned to look to the north east.

In plain sight rose the topsails and topgallants of a ship of the line. He recognised the cut at once.

Balthazar.

Captain Black Dick Cloughton.

This ship on which he had been court martialled now sailed to his rescue. The reaction was so severe he thought he'd lose the sight of his eyes once more.

The corvette had long since gone. *Zodiaque* had caught a wind that was failing as *Balthazar* came up. Soon the three British ships, the two frigates and ship of the line, wallowed in the sea, hove to.

Balthazar looked marvelous.

She looked solid, efficient, smart, with her double row of port lids triced up and her guns out. The scarlet gleam of marines on the poop, the wink and flash of gold lace on the quarterdeck, the strakes of yellow and black of her sides, and her sails gleaming with that saffron-white in the sunshine.

She wore the broad pendant of a commodore of the second class, that is, a commodore without a captain under him. Black Dick had said he would get his flag soon; this was a foretaste of his promotion to rear-admiral of the blue.

She was signalling, although the flags were difficult to read.

"That's our number," said Grey's voice. He had resumed his station as signals midshipman. "Do you require assistance?"

Fox felt like a good belly laugh. Trust Black Dick to make a joke out of blood and agony and death.

Lionel Grey had lost most of the usual polished smartness about him; his face was caked grey with powder smoke, a ball had ripped a white patch from his collar, his trousers were filthy; but Fox saw the line of his jaw and the look in his eyes and knew that Grey had come through all right. Carker, too, the good Carker, was already busying himself about the enormous number of tasks that must be done immediately.

"I believe we can manage," Fox said. "Ask for a surgeon."

"Aye aye, sir." Grey went to the signals locker, as calm as though this was a mere practice evolution. Men were lying about the deck, prostrate in complete exhaustion. The reaction was setting in. The frigate was a shambles. The bulwarks and gangways along the larboard waist had been beaten down. At least five eighteen pounders were toppled from their carriages. Grey had not had it easy.

"Oh, Mr. Grey. Make the signal: 'Assistance requested for *Lynx!*' "

"Aye aye, sir."

That should serve Toady Stone—if he was still alive.

Presently Captain Cloughton would send a boat, for all *Furieuse's* were smashed to chipwood. He would express the polite congratulations of the Navy in the polite formulae; but he was a fighting sailor and he would understand what had been going on here as the frigate endured her scourging of fire to hold a ship of the line away from the schemes of admiralty.

George Abercrombie Fox had set sail to dip his hands elbow deep in the golden plunder of the Spanish treasure ships. Instead he was surrounded by a wrecked vessel, with many good men dead, and with nothing to show for it. No flota. No prize. And *Zodiaque* had gone, vanished, leaving him with nothing.

All he had done was put up a good fight—and that was not only expected in the Royal Navy, anything less would not be tolerated. There were no promotions coming from this action.

Old Furry-arse.

She'd put up a fine show, for all that her bottom timbers were as rotten as that Josephine's teeth.

Captain Staunton was holding out his hand. The air rang with a strange deathly echoing silence after the broadsides.

"I'd like to offer you my congratulations, Mr. Fox. Damme if this ain't the finest action I ever did see."

It was an effort to be polite. "Thank you, sir. The whole ship's company fought magnificently." Platitudes, platitudes, with dead men and blood everywhere.

Fox reminded himself; there was always Percy Staunton, the favourite nephew of an admiral. There would be another time.

"Here comes a boat from *Balthazar* sir!" sang out Wilson.

Fox would have to look at the muster book, and discharge the dead men. He wondered how many of his men—*his* men—had survived. The reports would be coming in now. But there was the ship to put to rights, to rig, the men to bury over the side, and reports to write up—and a million other pressing tasks. The sun

150

shone, the gunsmoke had all blown away. There was much to do.

And all the effort and agony had been wasted because Captain Stone, his hated enemy Toady Stone, hadn't known how to handle a frigate in a fight with a two-decker.

"It's Captain Cloughton himself!" exclaimed Staunton.

Well, he must see to the proper compliments being paid when a commodore came over the side, even if the side was smashed to chipwood. Fox roused himself.

One thing—one thing—or two if he counted the fact he was still alive—*Furieuse* and her crew, Old Furry-Arse and her men, had fought damned well.

"We've a good ship," he said to Staunton. "A bloody good ship."